Four Historical Ro␣␣␣␣␣␣␣␣␣␣␣
on the Vibrant Gr␣␣␣␣␣␣␣␣␣

Prairie Summer BRIDES

The 12 Brides
of Summer
Book 1

MARGARET BROWNLEY, AMANDA CABOT,
VICKIE McDONOUGH, MICHELLE ULE

BARBOUR BOOKS
An Imprint of Barbour Publishing, Inc.

The Dog Days of Summer Bride © 2015 by Margaret Brownley
The Fourth of July Bride © 2015 by Amanda Cabot
The County Fair Bride © 2015 by Vickie McDonough
The Sunbonnet Bride © 2015 by Michelle Ule

ISBN 978-1-63409-528-0

All scripture quotations are taken from the King James Version of the Bible.

This book is a work of fiction. Names, characters, places, and incidents are either products of the author's imagination or used fictitiously. Any similarity to actual people, organizations, and/or events is purely coincidental.

Published by Barbour Books, an imprint of Barbour Publishing, Inc., P.O. Box 719, Uhrichsville, Ohio 44683, www.barbourbooks.com

Our mission is to publish and distribute inspirational products offering exceptional value and biblical encouragement to the masses.

 Member of the
Evangelical Christian
Publishers Association

Printed in the United States of America.

THE DOG DAYS OF SUMMER BRIDE

by Margaret Brownley

Chapter 1

Bee-Flat, Kansas
1883

Seven-year-old Timmy Crawford looked up from the piano. "I don't have enough fingers to play eighty-eight keys," he complained.

Marilee Davis smiled down at her young student and straightened the sheet music. "But you have more than enough to play these three notes." She demonstrated, calling the notes out loud. "C...D...E.... Now your turn."

Timmy poked each piano key with his forefinger as if squashing ants at a picnic.

"That's better," she said, not wanting to discourage the boy. "Now try again using *three* fingers."

This time Timmy got the fingering right but not the notes. Marilee was just about to correct him when her dog beat her to the punch. Shooting across the parlor in a black-and-white streak, his front paws landed on the ivory keys with a clash of dissonant chords.

Startled, Timmy cried out and almost fell off the piano stool.

Marilee pulled the dog away. "That's enough," she scolded. Naming him Mozart had been a mistake, though she called him Mo for short. All it did was put ideas in his furry head and make him think *he* was the music teacher instead of her.

"I'll take it from here." Her stern voice clearly showed she meant business. "Lie down!"

The dog's black tail drooped like a wilted flower. With a soft whimper he circled three times and flopped on the rug with an audible sigh. Muzzle lowered onto crossed paws, he gazed up at her with woeful brown eyes.

Mo didn't fool her a bit. Every doleful look and sorrowful gesture was an attempt to win her over, and nine times out of ten, it worked. But today her sympathy was with her young student, who stared at the dog with big round eyes.

"What's wrong with him?" Timmy asked. "How come he jumped up like that?" This was only Timmy's second lesson with Marilee, and he wasn't used to Mo's strange ways.

"Nothing's wrong with him," she said. *Much.* It was just her luck to get saddled with an eccentric, know-it-all cow dog. "He was just pointing out your wrong notes."

Mo usually let out a couple of warning barks before attacking the piano, allowing her to grab him before he did any harm. Today he sprang without warning.

"How does he know I played the wrong notes?"

"He can hear them. I think it hurts his ears." A tendril of blond hair escaped her tightly wound bun, and she brushed it away from her face. "So where were we?"

Timmy had taken lessons previously, but his original instructor had retired. The boy could barely play a scale let alone a simple melody, but that didn't keep his mother from insisting he was a gifted musician. Her opinion was based on him cutting his first tooth on a banjo case.

"Start from the beginning."

Timmy pulled his gaze away from the prone dog, swiped a strand of red hair out of his eyes, and scooted around to face the piano.

He really was a sweet boy, but with all his energy he would be better off playing ball with the other boys or cooling off in the nearby water hole.

Timmy hit another wrong note. Before Marilee could correct him, Mozart whimpered and covered his eyes with a paw. They were all three saved by the musical chimes of the grandfather clock. Mo rose on all fours, ears alert, tail wagging.

Marilee swore the animal could tell time. "That's enough for today, Timmy."

The boy didn't have to be told twice. He slipped off the piano stool and cautiously circled the dog.

"He won't hurt you," she said. Mo really was all bark and no bite. Usually, she put him outside during lessons, but this was Friday, and that was always the day the dog ran off to parts unknown.

She handed Timmy his music book along with a little bag

of penny candy. "See you next week. Don't forget to practice."

"I won't."

"And don't let the dog out—"

Her caution came too late. No sooner had Timmy opened the door than Mo took a flying leap outside.

By the time Marilee stormed after him, Mo was halfway down the road. "Mozart!" she called, hands at her waist. "Come back this minute. Do you hear me? Now."

Calling the dog back did no good. It never did.

"Sorry, Miss Davis."

"It's not your fault, Timmy." Nothing could keep that dog from running off to God knows where every blasted Friday. Not even the high fence in back which he tunneled under with the ease of a child crawling under a bed.

Shading her eyes against the late-afternoon sun, Marilee watched until Mo was but a speck in the distance. For the love of Betsy, what was wrong with that crazy dog? She gave it a good home with lots of attention. So why the disappearing act?

Where he went was anyone's guess. All Marilee knew was that when he came back he reeked like last week's fish dinner.

If the unpleasant odor wasn't bad enough, he also conveniently forgot everything she'd taught him and returned home with the manners of a hog. He jumped on her good furniture, begged at meals, and drank from unsavory places. Well, enough was enough!

Mo didn't know it yet, but his wandering days were about to end. Marilee meant to see that he stayed put even if she had to keep him under lock and key every weekend from here to doomsday.

After watching Timmy race down the road to his house, she stepped back inside and closed the door. He was the last student of the day. Her work was over, and she was free to do. . .what? She sighed. She had two students on Saturday, but the only bright spot in the weekend was Sunday worship.

Without Mo the house seemed empty, and she sat down at the piano to fill the loneliness the only way she knew how. Closing her eyes, she let her fingers fly up and down the keyboard with the ease of rippling water. She lost herself to Chopin, Mozart, and Beethoven. She loved what the music helped her remember.

She loved even more what it helped her forget.

Chapter 2

Blacksmith Jed Colbert pounded the heated horseshoe into shape. Sparks flew with each clank of steel. He couldn't remember a July so hot, and he paused for a moment to brush the perspiration from his forehead with his arm.

He held up the U-shaped metal piece with a pair of tongs. Satisfied, he tossed it onto a growing pile just as his friend Curly Madison walked in.

"Got any hub rings?" he asked.

"Over there." Jed slanted his head toward a wooden box. "Sure is hot."

"Yep, sure is," Curly said, pawing through the metal parts. "It's the dog days of summer all right." Anyone meeting Curly for the first time might think his name a joke, for he was bald as a newly shorn sheep, the unruly curls of his youth nothing but a fond memory.

Curly set two metal rings on the counter and dug into his trouser pocket for a handful of coins. "Where's Dynamite?"

he asked. Dynamite was Jed's black-and-white cow dog. "Still taking off on you?"

"Yep, every Monday like clockwork." Jed shook his head. "It's the craziest thing. I can't figure out where in the name of Sam Hill the fool dog goes. Who ever heard of a dog disappearing four out of seven days a week?"

Curly shrugged. "A dog gets something in his head and there's no changing it. Take Barney, for example." Barney was Curly's terrier. "It's been three years since I got him from his Catholic owner, and the dumb dog still refuses to eat on Fridays."

"Is that so?"

"Crazy, uh? Have you tried keeping the dog tied up?"

Jed picked up a piece of rope from his workbench. "Chewed right through it."

Curly shook his head. "It sure does look like he lives up to his name."

Jed tossed the rope back on the bench. "It wouldn't be so bad if he didn't come back smelling of perfume." Not that it was an unpleasant smell; not by any means. But it sure had caused him a wagonload of trouble.

The dog never failed to stink up the place, and the lavender-rose fragrance led Maizie Denton to jump to all the wrong conclusions. Now half the town considers him a womanizer and the other half wants to know his secret.

"Maizie still won't have anything to do with me. She's convinced I'm seeing other women."

Curly commiserated with a shake of his head. "Maybe you don't spend enough time with the dog. Maybe he seeks female companionship because he's lonely."

Jed hadn't considered that possibility. "I take him fishing every week. What more could he want?"

"Beats me." Curly palmed two coins on the counter and pocketed the rest. "I have enough trouble understandin' me own dog."

Just then a bark ripped through the air, and both men turned to the open double doors of the blacksmith shop.

"Speak of you-know-who," Curly said.

Dynamite rushed into the shop and greeted Jed with wagging tail. "It's about time you got here, boy." Jed scratched the dog behind both ears.

Woof!

"Whoo-eeee." Curly waved a hand in front of his nose. "It smells like a bordello in here."

"What did I tell you?" Jed said. "I've asked around town and no one, including Madam Bubbles, knows anything."

"All I can say is you better find out where Dyna spends his time or your love life will go to the dogs." Laughing at his own joke, Curly picked up the two metal hub rings and hobbled out of the shop. "See you at church," he called over his shoulder.

"See you." Jed stared down at Dyna. The dog had caused him nothing but trouble of late. It all started around four months ago. One day Dyna was a perfectly contented and normal dog. Then without warning, he started his disappearing act, and it had been one thing after another ever since.

Thanks to Maizie, his undeserved reputation as a philanderer had resulted in a decline of business. Some customers even went so far as to take their smithy needs to the next town.

The way things were going he'd soon be bankrupt, and all because of one dumb dog.

By the time Marilee arrived at church that hot Sunday morning, the only place left to sit was next to that awful womanizing blacksmith, Mr. Colbert.

Mrs. Pickwick, president of the women's auxiliary, had warned her and every other woman in town to stay away from him. To hear her tell it, the man was quite the lady-killer and no woman was safe from his roaming eye.

None of this particularly worried Marilee. She was quite capable of taking care of herself. At least where men were concerned. Still, sitting next to him in church could put a dent in her reputation. People tended to expect the highest moral standards from teachers, even those who taught music.

Bee Flat wasn't an unfriendly town, but neither did it greet strangers with open arms. Some matrons seemed especially wary of single, independent women.

Until Marilee was fully established as a music teacher and had proven herself trustworthy, she would have to watch her step where men were concerned.

Mr. Colbert turned to look at her as she slid onto the pew next to him. A crooked smile followed a quick nod of his head.

Up close, the man was quite the looker, and it was all she could do not to stare. Eyes the color of cornflowers looked out from a rugged square face. A brown swag of hair dipped from a side part, partially covering his brow. Dazzlingly white teeth showed from beneath parted lips, and for some odd reason, her cheeks grew warm beneath his steady gaze.

Since it would be rude not to acknowledge him, she nodded likewise but refused to favor him with even a polite smile. A woman couldn't be too careful around a man with his reputation. Looking away, she pulled off her kid gloves and accidently nudged his arm with her elbow.

"Sorry," she mumbled and focused her gaze on the organist to the right of the altar. Her trained ear picked out a popular ditty amid the more somber notes.

Mr. Colbert leaned sideways and whispered in her ear. "My Irish Molly-O," he said, naming the drinking song.

As if sharing a private joke, she met his smile with one of her own, and a moment of rapport sprang between them. She doubted that anyone else in the congregation had picked out the wayward tune. Not only did the organist have a sense of humor, but Mr. Colbert obviously had an ear for music. The clearing of a voice startled her into pulling her gaze away.

From the pew in front, Mrs. Pickwick shot her a

disapproving look. Her boat-like hat would have looked more at home sailing across the deep blue sea. It made Marilee's modest straw hat look almost too sedate in comparison.

No sooner had the last of the organ's chords faded away than Reverend Hampton took his place behind the pulpit. An older man with gray hair and sideburns, he wore a black robe with winglike sleeves. "Let us pray."

Closing her eyes, Marilee clasped her hands in her lap. During the silent prayer, she tried to concentrate on her blessings and not dwell on the lost dreams of her past.

"Amen," the minister said and promptly began to preach on the dog days of summer. "Tempers flare as the mercury rises," he expounded. "But what if we think of it as the inverted *God* days of summer? How would that affect our ways?"

It was an interesting concept, and Marilee was eager to hear more, but she was soon distracted. Next to her Mr. Colbert was sniffing like a bloodhound. Or was he sniffling?

She certainly hoped he wasn't coming down with something. The last thing she needed was to catch a summer cold. She tried scooting closer to the aisle but was already as close to the edge as possible.

Mr. Colbert leaned sideways and his shoulder touched hers. "Your perfume reminds me of my dog," he whispered.

Thinking she'd not heard right, she glanced at him. "I beg your pardon?" she whispered back.

"My dog," he said. "You smell like my dog."

Her mouth dropped open. Had she really heard what she thought she heard? She'd been warned about his womanizing ways, but nobody mentioned his lack of good manners.

He remained silent for the rest of the sermon except for an occasional sniffing sound. Whenever she thought it safe to do so, she stole a glance at him. Invariably, she found him looking back. At such times she quickly turned her head and continued to seethe. Like his dog, indeed!

The congregation stood for the closing hymn. As the last organ chord faded away, she jumped to her feet and scurried up the aisle.

Outside, she was stopped by the mother of one of her students who anxiously inquired about her daughter's progress. Since it was neither the time nor place to discuss such matters, Marilee responded in general terms.

"Yes, Charlene is"—*a sweet girl but musically impaired*—"coming along quite nicely," she said. "Be sure to have her practice."

If it wasn't for mothers seeing genius where none existed, most music teachers would be out of business. Of course, the word *genius* was never used in describing female children. *Domesticated* was the best a girl could expect. The ability to play the piano was considered almost as important in landing a future husband as learning to cook and sew.

Not that it had helped Marilee. If anything, her ambition to play in an orchestra had proven to be a detriment in matters of the heart. No man was interested in a woman with such lofty ambitions. At the age of twenty-four she'd reached a dead end in both a marriage prospect and her dream of playing in a symphony orchestra.

While calming the anxieties of yet another student's mother, she saw Mr. Colbert step outside the church and head her way. Since he stood taller than most of the other men, it was hard not to notice his commanding presence.

He caught up to her just as she reached her springboard wagon. "Your glove," he said.

"Oh." She took the offered glove from him. Perhaps he wasn't completely without manners. Since he towered over her by a good six inches she was forced to look up. "Thank you."

"I fear we may have gotten off on the wrong foot," he said.

She drew on her glove and wriggled her fingers into the silky depths. "The wrong foot?"

"In church." He hesitated a moment. "I didn't mean to offend you."

"You mean by telling me I smelled like your dog?" she said, her voice cool.

He lowered his head and rubbed the back of his neck. "I meant it in a good way," he said and grinned.

She wasn't sure if it was the sheepish look or the crooked smile, but her irritation melted away like wax from a candle. "In that case, I guess there was no harm done," she said.

A look of relief crossed his face. "I don't think we've ever been formally introduced." He doffed his wide-brim hat. "I'm Jed Colbert."

Behind him Mrs. Pickwick stopped to stare, her pointed face dark with disapproval.

Marilee drew in her breath. "Miss Davis," she said, careful to keep her expression neutral for the auxiliary president's sake. "Now if you'll excuse me. . ."

"Sorry. Didn't mean to keep you."

Scrambling up to the driver's seat as quickly as decorum would allow, she gathered the reins in hand. "Good day, Mr. Colbert."

He raked her over with bold regard. Tipping his broad-brimmed hat, he flashed a smile. "I like it," he called up to her.

"Like what?"

"Why, your perfume, of course. My dog likes it, too."

She snapped her mouth shut. *Impertinent man!* Such a personal comment was bad enough, but to say it out loud so anyone could hear was beyond the pale.

With an indignant toss of her head, she shook the reins hard and drove off.

Chapter 3

Jed stood on the bank of the Bee Flat River. Bamboo fishing rod held over his shoulder, he brought it forward with a snap of the wrist. The line sailed overhead and hook and sinker hit the water with a splash.

Rod in hand, he settled onto a grassy spot. Nearby, Dyna sniffed the bucket of fish.

He came back Friday doused in perfume, but today only the faintest aroma of lavender-rose remained. Still, it was enough to trigger the memory of a pretty round face, big blue eyes, and hair that looked as light and soft as corn silk.

The perfume smelled a whole lot better on the music teacher than it did on Dyna, that's for certain and sure. It crossed his mind that she might know something about Dyna's disappearing act, but he soon discounted that idea. A fine lady like her wouldn't look twice at a big clumsy cow dog like Dyna.

He'd noticed her in church before, but this morning

was the first he'd seen her up close. She was one of those uptight women from the east and obviously didn't think much of him.

He just wished she hadn't looked at him like he had rabies or something. Not that he blamed her.

There was probably a better way to say *"You smell like my dog."* The memory made him wince. Since being on the outs with the ladies, his manners had grown as rusty as an old water pump. It was scary to think he was better able to talk to an animal than a member of the opposite sex.

As if to guess his thoughts, Dyna let out a short, sharp bark.

"Shh. You'll scare away the fish." He picked up a stick and tossed it. Dyna bounded after it, ears back. Instead of retrieving it he stopped to sniff around a huge cottonwood. The stick forgotten, Dyna began to dig, dirt flying from beneath his front paws.

A clod of dirt landed in Jed's lap, and the smell of damp earth absorbed the last of the lavender-rose fragrance. "Watch it," he said, but the dog paid him no heed. He just kept digging.

Jed reeled his line in slowly and gave his bait a jerk. He didn't even know why Miss Davis was on his mind. She obviously wanted nothing to do with him. Nor he with her. He'd had his fill of female troubles in recent months. So what did he need a stuck-up music teacher for?

Dyna nudged his arm. When he failed to respond, the

dog dropped something into his lap and barked.

"Shh. I told you—"

Thinking Dyna had dug up a bone, Jed lifted the soil-caked object between thumb and forefinger. Nope. Not a bone. He shook off the dirt, blinked, and shook some more. "What in blazes?"

He reeled in his line and set his pole on the ground. He then reexamined the packet. This time there was no question. Dyna had dug up a stack of money bound by a paper band.

Dyna ran to the hole he'd dug underneath the tree and looked back as if to say *what are you waiting for?* Jed jumped to his feet and followed. Dropping down on his knees, he reached into a rotted gunnysack and pulled out a second packet.

Hauling the sack out of the hole, he ripped it all the way open and his jaw dropped. There had to be at least fifty grand staring him in the face. He pushed back his hat and shook his head. Holy mackerel!

Chapter 4

Marilee bumped into Mrs. Pickwick at Henderson's Dry Goods early that Monday morning.

"How lovely to see you," Marilee said with a smile. With all her faults, the woman had been kind enough to take Marilee under her wing when she first arrived in town. It was Mrs. Pickwick's brother-in-law who rented her the house.

"You, too." Mrs. Pickwick ran a jeweled hand across a bolt of calico. "You are coming to the Tuesday Afternoon Club meeting, aren't you? I thought we would discuss what book we want to read next."

"I'll be there," Marilee said.

Mrs. Pickwick lowered her voice. "Was that Mr. Colbert I saw you talking to?"

"Mr. Colbert?" Just saying his name put her in a state of confusion. One moment he had insulted her and the next. . . "Oh, you mean in church?"

"Yes, and after."

"I left my glove behind, and he kindly returned it."

The woman stared down her pointed nose. "Well, you better watch your step. As you know, he broke Maizie Denton's heart with his womanizing ways."

Oh, yes, Marilee did know that. Maizie and her broken heart had been the main topic of conversation for weeks and had taken up most of the Tuesday Afternoon Club meetings.

Thanking the woman for her concern, Marilee paid for her goods and walked out of the store with her basket of purchases flung over her arm.

At the end of the street a crowd of people was gathered by the windmill. A man stood on a soapbox talking through a megaphone. The bulk of his body told her it was Mayor Blackmon. Thinking it was a political rally, she set her basket into the wagon, anxious to get home before the heat of the day.

Just as she started to climb up to the driver's seat she heard an all-too-familiar bark. The sound came from the direction of the crowd. Shading her eyes against the sun she scanned the area. Was that Mozart sitting next to the soapbox? She couldn't be certain, but it sure did look like him. Of course most cow dogs looked alike. Still. . .

Only one way to find out. Reaching for her parasol, she popped it open and hurried toward the knot of people.

Standing on tiptoes, she craned her neck to see over

the crowd. Next to the mayor stood none other than the blacksmith—Mr. Colbert, looking tall and handsome and very much in command. At his feet sat a black-and-white dog with exactly the same markings as Mo. If it wasn't him then it had to be his twin.

Closing her parasol, she inched her way through the crowd to get a better look. Marilee never thought to have something in common with the likes of Mr. Colbert, but it seemed they both owned similar dogs.

The mayor patted Mr. Colbert on the back. He barely reached the blacksmith's shoulders, but what he lacked in height he made up for in width.

"If it wasn't for Jed, here, and his dog, we might never have found the money," he said, and the crowd applauded.

Marilee waited for the clapping to stop before turning to the man next to her. "What's this about money?" she asked.

"The bank was robbed two years ago, and they just now found the stolen loot," he replied.

"Oh, I see." Marilee shouldered her way to the front of the crowd.

"As a token of our appreciation," the mayor was saying, "It's my pleasure to present this check for—"

Just then the dog looked up, spotted Marilee, and barked. He leaped toward the crowd in a streak of flying fur and practically knocked her down, his dirty paws all over her skirt.

She rubbed his head. "Mo, is that you?" Phew. What a dreadful odor. A wagonload of fish on a hot day couldn't smell worse. "What are you doing here?"

She looked up to find the mayor and Mr. Colbert staring at her. "Excuse me, ma'am, but I'm trying to make a presentation here," the mayor said. "The dog is a hero."

A hero? Mo?

"There must be some sort of mistake," she said. "This is my dog and—"

The mayor reared back and looked at Colbert. "What is she talking about?"

"That's what I want to know," Colbert said. "Dyna, come here, boy."

Much to Marilee's chagrin, her dog turned and ran to the soapbox. He plopped his behind next to Colbert, and his tail swept the ground like the broom of a fastidious housewife.

"Excuse me, sir," she called politely, not wishing to make a scene. She walked up to the soapbox. "But I do believe that's my dog."

As if to concur, Mo rose on all fours and moved to her side.

The mayor looked from Colbert to Marilee and back to Colbert. "Is that true?"

"Of course it's not true," Colbert said. "Dyna, come here, boy." The dog obeyed.

The mayor scratched his head. "The reward is supposed

to go to the dog's owner."

"That would be me," Colbert and Marilee said in unison. They locked gazes.

"The dog is mine," she said. "His name is Mozart, but I call him Mo."

A look of annoyance crossed Colbert's face. "I'm afraid you're mistaken, Miss Davis. His name is Dynamite—Dyna for short."

Just then Marilee's student, Timmy Crawford, stepped forward. "That's Miss Davis's dog."

"Nonsense," yelled a baldheaded man. "That's Jed's dog."

Others jumped into the fray, taking sides. Soon it seemed as if the whole town was up in arms.

"That dog belongs to Miss Davis," a student's mother exclaimed. "And that's that!"

"Are you out of your cotton-pickin' mind? That's Jed's hound."

"Jed's hound my—"

"Hold it," the mayor pleaded. He held his hands up, palms out. "I'm sure we can settle this matter in an amicable fashion."

"I'll show you amicable," a thin man with a bushy beard yelled. "It's Jed's dog, and that's all there is to it. He owes me money and promised to pay me out of the reward."

The man next to him refused to back down. "I'm telling you that's Miss Davis's dog."

With that he punched the other man in the jaw.

No sooner had his knuckles made contact when fists began to fly. A baby let out a wail in high C, and his mother ran for cover. Thinking it was playtime, Mo barked joyfully as he pranced around two men rolling on the ground.

Marilee winced at the sound of pounding flesh. "Stop," she cried. "Please stop!" But her pleas fell on deaf ears. She glanced around for Mr. Colbert, but he was busy pulling two battling men apart.

The skirmish brought the sheriff on the run. He yelled for everyone to hold their horses and when that failed to get the desired results, he pulled out his pistol, pointed the muzzle upward, and fired three shots.

That did the trick. Men rolled off each other groaning and rubbing sore jaws.

The sheriff holstered his gun and his horseshoe mustache twitched. "What's going on here?"

Everyone started talking at once.

"She—"

"He—"

"One at a time!" the sheriff yelled. He pointed to Marilee. "What's this about you trying to steal Jed's dog?"

"I am *not* stealing his dog." Her voice shook with indignation, as did her parasol. "He's *my* dog. He was a stray, and I took him in and—"

"That dog ain't no stray. He's Jed's dog!" yelled someone from the crowd.

"Quiet!" the sheriff barked. This time he turned to Colbert. "Is this your dog or ain't it?"

"It's my dog, all right," Colbert said. "You know it is. Raised him from a puppy."

The sheriff circled the dog. "Well, it sure does look like Dynamite."

"Only it's not," Marilee said, fearing the tide had turned against her.

The sheriff pushed his hat to the back of his head and looked at her with narrowed eyes. "Okay, I'll give you two choices. One, we can split the dog in two and you'll each get half—"

Marilee gasped. "That. . .that's a horrid idea!"

The sheriff shrugged. "Worked for King Solomon."

Colbert glared at him, obviously in no mood for jokes. "What's the second choice?"

"The second choice is to put the dog in jail until we figure out his rightful owner."

Marilee shuddered at the thought of her dear sweet dog behind bars. "That would be downright cruel."

"And it still doesn't tell us who gets the reward money," someone yelled.

The sheriff took Mo by the collar. "I guess that will have to wait till these two figure out who owns what."

"Wait." Marilee moistened her lips. "You can give Mr. Colbert the reward. I'll take the dog."

"I don't care a fiddle about the money," Mr. Colbert

snapped. "All I care about is Dyna."

"His name is Mozart."

Mr. Colbert leaned forward until his nose practically touched hers. "What kind of dumb name is that for a—"

The sheriff stepped between them. "All right, you two, that's enough. We're gonna handle this in a democratic way. We'll let Dyna—Mozart—whatever his name, decide who he wants to go home with."

Mr. Colbert folded his arms across his chest. "Fine by me."

"Fine by me, too," she said, glaring up at him. *Harrumph.* The man looked so sure Mo would choose him. He would soon find out otherwise. Oh, yes, indeed he would!

"All right then," the sheriff said. "Take ten paces back, both of you." He spread his arms to demonstrate.

Marilee counted her steps and turned; Colbert did likewise. They faced each other on the dusty road like two unflinching gunfighters about to draw their weapons. Their gazes clashed like swords.

"A silver dollar says the lady wins," the owner of the livery stables shouted.

No sooner were the words out of his mouth than bets flew back and forth like swarming bees.

Marilee tapped her foot. She didn't have time for this nonsense. It was hot, and she just wanted to take Mo home. She raised her parasol over her head and waited.

"Quiet!" the sheriff yelled at last with a wave of his arms. He waited for the crowd to fall silent. "This is how it's gonna work. You'll each call the dog by name. You have thirty seconds to get him to come to you and no more." He pulled his watch out of his vest pocket and held up a hand. "We'll let the lady go first."

Marilee patted her leg. "Come here, Mo. Come on, boy. Let's go home."

Mo wagged his tail and barked, but didn't move, not even when she promised to give him a nice juicy bone.

The sheriff dropped his hand to indicate her time was up and swung his attention to Colbert. "Your turn."

Colbert touched the brim of his hat as if to say this is how it's done. He then turned to the dog. "Come, Dyna. Let's go home." He promised to take the dog fishing and play ball.

The dog cocked his head and his ears perked up, but he stubbornly remained in place.

The sheriff shrugged. "It looks like the dog goes to the jailhouse with me."

Alarmed, Marilee tossed Mr. Colbert a beseeching glance. Her voice was shaking so much she could hardly get the words out. "Please, there must be another way."

Colbert's eyes were as dark as the night sky, and for several long moments no one spoke. "Dyna can go home with the lady," he said at last. "Least till we have time to figure this out."

"What about the money?" the mayor asked.

"Hold on to it for now," Colbert said. He then stalked

away, and the crowd quickly dispersed.

Marilee walked over to Mo, who didn't look the least bit guilty for all the trouble he'd caused. "Let's get you home. You need a bath."

Waving the fishy smell away, she grabbed the dog by the collar and led him to her buckboard.

Chapter 5

By noon the next day it seemed as if half the women in town had beaten a path to Marilee's door. Mrs. Pickwick arrived a little after one in the afternoon.

Mo looked up from where he was napping. He gave a halfhearted wag of his tail and laid his head down again.

"I swear, every summer is hotter than the last," Mrs. Pickwick said, cooling herself off with a vigorous wave of her fan.

Marilee commiserated with a nod. "Do sit, and I'll get you a glass of lemonade."

Instead of sitting, Mrs. Pickwick followed Marilee into the kitchen, shaking her feathered head like a clucking hen. "Everyone in town is talking about the confusion with the dog. Who ever heard of such a thing?"

"It's crazy, I know." Marilee filled two glasses with lemonade and set them on the table. She then followed this with a plate of freshly baked macaroons.

"What are you going to do?" Mrs. Pickwick asked as she sat at the kitchen table and helped herself to a cookie.

Marilee took a seat opposite her. "I've been praying about it, and I've decided it's only right that I return Mo to Mr. Colbert."

Mrs. Pickwick practically choked. "Right? How could that be right?" She daintily wiped crumbs away from the corner of her mouth. "Why, you love that dog. And you take such good care of him."

"Yes, but I've only had him for a few months, whereas Mr. Colbert raised him from a puppy." Now that she knew where Mo went every week, she couldn't in good conscience claim Mo as hers. Through no fault of their own, she and the blacksmith had both been duped.

Mrs. Pickwick reached for another cookie. "If you ask me, it's a crying shame that you have to give him up."

"Yes, it is," Marilee said and took a sip of lemonade. She set her glass down, her mind made up. "But I've been thinking about what Reverend Hampton said about the *God* days of summer, and I know it's the right thing to do." If only it didn't hurt so much.

A familiar bark drew Jed's gaze from his workbench just as Dynamite bounced into the shop. A smile spreading across his face, Jed set his hammer down and stooped to give his dog a proper welcome.

"What are you doing here?" he asked. On a weekday no less.

For answer, Dynamite licked his hand, his tail whipping back and forth like a trainman's lantern.

A shadow blocked the open door and Jed looked up. He suddenly found himself drowning in the music teacher's pretty blue eyes.

Flustered, he stood. It wasn't often that such a lady set foot in his shop. "Miss Davis."

It was hotter than blazes, but she looked as cool as a cucumber in a blue skirt and lace shirtwaist that showed off her feminine curves to full advantage. Her outfit was topped by a straw hat tilted at a perky angle.

"Mr. Colbert," she said, matching his wary demeanor.

He reached for a rag on his workbench and mopped his forehead. "What brings you here?"

"I've been. . .thinking."

"Go on."

"It seems we've been sharing the same dog. I believe Mo. . .uh. . .has been taking advantage of us."

He'd been thinking along those same lines himself. It was the only thing that made sense.

"Seems that way."

"Since I've only had him for a few months and you've raised him from a puppy, it seems only right that you claim ownership."

He rubbed the back of his neck. "Well, now." Praise the Lord, his troubles were about to end. He could now claim the reward money and maybe even repair his undeserved reputation. Who knows? Once the whole story came out, maybe even Maizie would give him a second chance.

"That's mighty thoughtful of you, Miss Davis. Sure do appreciate it." He just wished he didn't feel so doggone awful. It was obvious she cared deeply for Dyna, just as he did.

She moistened her lips. "Do you mind if I say good-bye to him?"

"No, no, of course not. Go right ahead."

She stooped next to Dyna and rubbed his head. "I'm going to miss you, Mo, but this is where you belong."

Her voice broke, and much to Jed's dismay, her eyes filled with tears. He felt in his pockets. Blast it all. Of all the times not to have a clean handkerchief on him.

He moved toward her meaning to comfort her. Take her in his arms even. Make her tears vanish. But before he had a chance to do any of those things, she rose to her feet, lifted her chin as if trying to control her emotions, and backed toward the door.

"I—I better go," she stammered. Without another word, she turned and dashed out of the shop.

"Wait!" He chased after her, catching up to her just as she settled in the seat of her buckboard.

"Feel free to visit him," he called up to her. *Every day if you want.*

She blinked as if trying to clear her vision. "What?"

"Dyna. . .Mo." Whatever his name. "You can visit him any time."

She shook her head, and he could see her struggling for control. "I don't think that's a good idea. It would only prolong the pain. But. . .but thank you anyway. It was very kind of you to offer. Just. . .just take good care of him." She reached for the reins and drove off.

Watching her he felt awful. The worst. Lower than dirt. He didn't do anything wrong, but he sure did feel like a heel.

He blew out his breath. That crazy dog would be the death of him yet. He spun around and stalked into his shop.

"Now look what you've gone and done, you dumb dog." He stopped and looked around. "Dyna?" When that got no response, he called, "Mo?"

He looked under his workbench and behind the forge, but the dog was nowhere to be found.

Chapter 6

Arriving home, Marilee hardly had time to remove her gloves and hat when she heard the bark.

"Oh, no. God, please don't let that be—"

But it was. No sooner had she opened the door than Mo bounced inside and took up residence on her green velvet sofa.

"Mo. Down, now."

Mo hopped off the sofa and pranced around barking. Marilee dropped down to her knees and ran her hands through the dog's soft, fragrant fur. He still smelled pleasant from his earlier bath.

"You've got to go back, Mo. You can't stay here." The longer he stayed, the harder it would be to let him go. The problem was she didn't have time to take him back. A student was due to arrive at any minute. "As soon as I'm finished here, I'm taking you back to Mr. Colbert. Is that clear?"

A knock on the door announced her student's arrival, and she hurried to let the child in.

Jed locked the door to his shop. His horse, Marshal, greeted him with a wicker. He ran his hand along the bay's neck. Thoughts of Miss Davis continued to plague him. If only she hadn't looked so devastated when saying good-bye to her. . .his. . .dog.

"Jed. Yoo-hoo!"

Much to his surprise, it was Maizie Denton, who hadn't talked to him since the day Dyna first came home reeking of perfume. He waited for her to cross the street. She was a tall, slender woman with blazing red hair and lively green eyes. She stopped and gazed at him over the saddle of his horse.

"I heard all about the fight over Dyna," she said. "It seems I jumped to all the wrong conclusions."

He tightened the cinch on the saddle. "Oh?" He frowned. "What conclusions were those?"

"I accused you of seeing other women." She did her fluttering-eyelash thing. "All the time it was your dog carrying on."

He frowned. "I tried to tell you."

"Yes, you did, and I'm really sorry." Lips pouted, she gave him a beseeching look. "Will you ever forgive me?" she asked in a high-pitched voice usually saved for babies and puppies. When he didn't answer, she persisted. "Well?

Do you or don't you?"

"Do I or don't I what?"

She looked at him all funny-like. "Forgive me."

"Sure. Why not?" he said. He wasn't one to hold a grudge, but he was still irritated at her for spreading rumors and ruining his reputation.

It was obvious she wanted him to say more, and when he didn't, uncertainty crossed her face. "You don't look like you forgive me."

"We'll talk about this later, Maizie." He splayed his hands in apology. "I've got to go and find Mo."

"Who's Mo?"

"What?"

"You said you had to find Mo?"

"I meant. . .Dyna. I have to find Dyna."

Her forehead creased. "I have to say you're acting very strange," she said, looking hurt.

For the second time that day he felt like a heel. None of this was Maizie's fault. Anyone smelling perfume would naturally assume he was seeing other women. If only she'd trusted him enough to believe him. Or at least trusted his faith in God enough to know he wouldn't lie to her.

"I just have a lot on my mind, is all. We'll talk later."

"When later?" she persisted.

"Tomorrow."

Satisfied that he had placated her, he untied his horse from the hitching post and mounted. He avoided her eyes as he turned his horse and galloped out of town.

No sooner had her student left when Marilee heard a rap at the door. Mo jumped up with wagging tail.

"Sit, Mo."

Mo sat, but only long enough for her to open the door. He then sprang past her and greeted the visitor like a long-lost friend.

"Mr. Colbert!" she uttered. "You shouldn't have come all the way out here. I would have brought him back."

He looked up from petting the dog. "Jed."

"What?"

"My name's Jed."

"Marilee," she said without thinking, and he immediately repeated her name as if committing it to memory.

Normally she would object to such familiarity. But she liked the way her name sounded when he said it—like a rolled piano chord.

"Please come in," she said, a bit more primly than she intended. No sense keeping him standing on the porch for all the neighbors to see.

He straightened and stepped inside, his long lean form seeming to fill her parlor. The room suddenly seemed too small. He knocked against the kerosene lamp, catching it before it fell to the floor. Turning, he almost sent a music box flying off the low table.

"Sorry," he said, catching the music box just in time,

only to knock against a porcelain figurine. Straightening, he glanced around as if checking for other obstacles. Clearing his throat, he ran a finger around his collar. "About the dog. . ."

"I had nothing to do with his return," she said. "He just showed up on my doorstep."

"Yes, well it seems we have a problem. But I think I've come up with a solution."

"A solution?"

His gaze locked with hers. He really did have nice eyes. Kind eyes. "We could go on just like before. He's yours from Monday to Friday. The rest of the time he's mine."

She bit her lower lip. "That doesn't seem fair. You only get him for the weekends."

He shrugged. "Not much I can do about that. He made the schedule, not me."

She tucked a strand of hair behind her ear. "It does seem like a rather strange arrangement, don't you think?"

"It's no different than what we've been putting up with for the last few months."

"I suppose. But I do want you to have the reward money. You had Mo first."

"Dyna," he said. "His name is Dynamite."

She gave her head a slight shake. "Such an unpleasant name for such a sweet and gentle dog, don't you think?"

"Sweet and gentle? He's a herding dog. Nothing sweet and gentle about that. Put him with a herd of cattle and we're talking Dyna the Terrible."

She glanced at Mo and gasped. He knew better than to sit on the sofa. "Mo, down. Now."

Jed frowned. "Is there something wrong with the sofa, ma'am?"

"What?"

"The sofa. You were worried about the dog sitting on it. Thought maybe a leg was loose or something. I'll be glad to fix it if you like."

"There's nothing wrong with the sofa. I just don't want him getting his fur and muddy paws all over the cushions."

Jed frowned. "I guess that means he doesn't get to sleep on your bed either," he said.

"Certainly not. No one gets to sleep—"

He raised a brow, waiting for her to continue. A moment of awkward silence passed between them before she cleared her throat. "Dogs don't belong on the furniture," she said.

"And Dyna agrees to your rules?" he asked, clearly astonished.

"Dyna doesn't, but Mo does," she said.

He surprised her by laughing. He really was a handsome man when he wasn't scowling. "That's all we need, a dog with a dual personality."

She laughed, too. She couldn't help herself.

He stared at her for a moment before seeming to catch himself. "I won't keep you any longer." As he backed toward the door, he bumped into the hat tree, catching it before it toppled over.

Suddenly she didn't want him to go. Or maybe she didn't want to face yet another night alone. "I was just about to have supper. Would you care to join me? I have plenty."

He looked surprised by the offer, but no more surprised than she was for making it. "That's mighty generous of you, ma'am. If it's not too much trouble."

"N–no trouble at all." Now look what she'd gone and done. Mrs. Pickwick would have a fit if she knew she'd invited the womanizing Mr. Colbert to supper.

"Make yourself at home," she said.

She left him alone with Mo while she escaped to the kitchen. It had been a long time since she'd entertained a gentleman guest. Not that he was a gentleman guest, of course. At least not in the full sense of the word, so there really was no reason for her heart to bounce around like a rubber ball.

Hands on her chest to still the thumps, she chided herself for behaving like a silly schoolgirl. Now where was she? Oh, yes. The stew. . .

Chapter 7

After nearly knocking the lamp over for a second time, Jed looked for a place to sit. Not brave enough to risk his bulk to the spindly chairs, he sat on the only sincere if not altogether stable piece of furniture in the room: the sofa.

He wasn't usually so clumsy, but the furniture seemed to crowd in like animals at a water hole. About the only thing he hadn't knocked against was the bookshelf, which contained at least half as many books as the lending library across town.

Pulling off his hat, he set it on the cushion next to him and raked his fingers through his hair. Confound it. He needed a haircut. Why hadn't he thought about that before?

The delicious smell wafting from the kitchen made him forget his hair. Whatever she was cooking sure did smell good, and his stomach rumbled. Should he join her in the kitchen or wait to be called? The lady seemed to be a stickler for rules, so he better wait.

Leaning forward, he rubbed his hands between his knees. That's when he noticed his dusty boots against the pristine red carpet. He lifted one foot and then another, wiping each toe box in turn on the back of his trouser legs.

"I'm lucky the lady didn't toss *me* in the bathtub," he muttered. He should never have come here straight from the shop.

As if to commiserate, Dyna sat up, ears perked. *Ruff!*

"You got that right. Dealing with women is rough all right." Especially one who was such a lady.

"Supper's ready," Marilee called.

Standing, he straightened his vest. He walked into the kitchen just as she set the second plate of stew on the table—and what a table it was. Candles and fresh flowers shared space with gold-trimmed china dishes and sparkling glassware.

Dyna padded after him and sniffed at the dish on the floor before gulping down his food.

"It sure does smell good," he said. "Real good." He hadn't had any honest-to-goodness home cooking since Maizie stopped talking to him.

He held her chair for her before taking a seat opposite. Dyna licked his plate clean and flopped down on the floor between them, resting his head on crossed paws.

Jed stared down at the confusing amount of silverware.

Why anyone needed three forks and two spoons he couldn't imagine.

"Would you care to say the blessing?" she asked.

"Sure thing, ma'am." He might not know which spoon was which, but he knew how to talk to the Lord. He lowered his head and thanked God for the company, the food, and all that was good in the world. "Amen."

"Amen," she said. She picked up her napkin and, giving it a dainty little shake, spread it across her lap.

Following her lead, he picked up his own napkin and, forgoing the dainty part, set it on his lap still folded.

"If you don't mind my asking," he said, helping himself to a roll, "what brought you to Bee Flat?"

"Actually I ended up here by accident." She buttered her roll like an artist painting on a canvas. "I was on my way to San Francisco. When I came to the end of the train line, I couldn't find a stage or wagon train willing to haul my piano the rest of the way."

He stabbed a piece of meat with his fork. "So you decided to stay."

She shrugged. "At the time, it seemed like God's will. What better place for a music teacher than a town named Bee Flat?"

His fork stilled between the plate and his mouth. "I'm afraid I don't see the connection."

"B flat. It's a musical note."

"Don't know much about music," he admitted. "Don't

know a B flat from a bullhorn."

"But you have an ear for it," she said. "You did pick out that ditty in church."

She sounded impressed and that surprised him. Surely it didn't take any special talent to recognize a tune. "I always wanted to play an instrument but never got around to it." He took a bite of his meat and chewed. Something occurred to him and he chuckled.

"What's so funny?" she asked.

"Actually, Bee Flat has nothing to do with music. It was named after a real person. Her name was Beatrice Flat. Bee for short. Story is that her covered wagon broke down on the way to Oregon. She refused to lighten the load by parting with her books, so she and her husband abandoned their plans to travel west and stayed here. They lived in a soddy and founded the town. Thanks to Bee Flat the lending library was built first and the rest of the town sprang up around it." Not that he was a book person, himself, but judging by the number of books in the parlor, Marilee was an avid reader.

Her eyes shone bright in the soft yellow light. "I can understand someone not wanting to give up her books," she said.

"I reckon you can." He tried to think if anything he owned meant that much to him. Maybe his horse. And of course, Dyna. He buttered his roll with the same broad movements it took to feed the hogs.

"What's in San Francisco?" he asked.

"Music. Concert halls," she said. "I thought it would be a good place for a music teacher to live."

"Doesn't Boston have concert halls?"

"How do you know I'm from Boston?" she asked.

If the way she pronounced her As didn't give her away, her dress and manners surely did. "Lucky guess," he said.

"My mother was British, and my father was a military man stationed at Fort Warren."

"Is that right?" That explained a lot. The British were as rigid in deportment as the military. No wonder the dog wasn't allowed to sit on the furniture. "So why'd you leave?"

She hesitated as if she wasn't certain she wanted to answer the question. "I won a blind contest and the prize was an audition for the Boston Symphony Orchestra. It was a dream come true."

The closest Jed had ever come to hearing an orchestra was when Bruce Miller played his mouth organ along with Jake Randall's fiddle and Bob Henshaw's washboard. "What's a blind contest?"

"Contestants were required to play behind a curtain so the judges couldn't show favoritism to friends or relatives. No one knew I was a woman until the winner was announced. When my name was called it caused quite a stir."

He grinned. "I can imagine. But they let you audition, right?"

She shook her head. "Women aren't allowed to play in the orchestra no matter how well they play. I was accused of duping the judges, and it made the front page of the *Boston Globe*."

"That's. . .that's terrible."

"The worst part is, I was betrothed to a man running for his second term as senator. He lost the election because of me."

He blinked. A senator? She was engaged to a senator? "Surely he didn't blame you."

She shrugged. "Wouldn't you?"

He shook his head and covered her hand with his own. "I'm sorry."

Her cheeks turned pink as she glanced down at his hand, and he quickly removed it. An awkward silence passed between them before she asked, "What about you? How long have you lived in Bee Flat?"

Grateful for the change of subject, he reached for another roll. "Moved here from Austin, Texas, when I was seventeen. I was a wild one, and my pa sent me here to live with my uncle and learn the blacksmithing trade. When my uncle died, I took over the shop." He mopped up his plate with his roll.

"A wild one, uh?" she said. She flashed him the prettiest smile, but there was something in her manner that alerted him, a sudden reserve perhaps. Maybe she regretted being so candid about her past. His cousin accused him of being insensitive. In reality he simply didn't pick up on nuances. He needed things stated flat out, plain and simple. But oddly enough, tonight he was aware of every smile, every voice inflection, and every expression that crossed her pretty round face.

They chatted for the rest of the meal. She talked about growing up in Boston and how a German immigrant had taught her to play the piano in exchange for free room and board in her parents' home.

"The problem with living with your piano teacher is you couldn't get away with not practicing," she said.

He talked about growing up in Texas. He was only nine when his mother died, and that's when he started playing truant and getting into mischief.

"You must have missed her very much," she said.

"Yeah, I did."

Somehow the talk turned to Dyna. "When he came back smelling of perfume, everyone thought I'd been with other women," he explained. "Even though I hadn't."

"I'm so sorry." This time it was her hand that sought his. He stared down at the lily white hand with the long tapered fingers, and his looked like a big clumsy paw in comparison.

He offered to help clean up afterward, but she refused to let him. So there really was nothing left to do but take his leave. But he didn't want the evening to end. He couldn't remember having such a good time.

"Thank you for the grub," he said. Since the word hardly did the meal justice he quickly corrected himself. "Eh. . .stew. You're a fine cook."

She smiled again and glints of golden light replaced the earlier sadness in her eyes.

"Don't worry," she said. "I'll take good care of him."

His mind drew a blank. "Him?"

"Mo. . .uh."

"Dyna," he said.

The dog stood between them looking from one to the other as if waiting for them to make up their minds what to call him.

She followed him out of the kitchen. Careful not to knock anything over, he plucked his hat from the sofa and set it on his head.

"Did you bring all this stuff with you on the train?" he asked, glancing around the room.

She shook her head. "My mother arranged for it to be shipped here. She insists that no one can be a proper lady without a properly furnished parlor."

"Well, then. . ." His gaze drifted to the piano. Would it be rude to ask her to play? Probably.

She opened the door and a whoosh of air teased the draperies and ruffled Dyna's fur.

He stooped to pet him. "See you on Friday, buddy," he said. "Don't forget."

"I'll see that he doesn't," she said.

He stood and touched a finger to the brim of his hat. "Mighty obliged."

No sooner had he stepped outside than she whispered a good-night and closed the door. The soft prairie breeze had cooled the air, and the sky was a mass of twinkling stars.

Overhead, Orion arched his arrow. Nearby was the constellation Canis Major—Orion's hunting dog. Jed didn't know much about music, but he knew about the stars. There wasn't a whole lot to do on a lonely night but gaze at the sky.

Just as he reached his horse, the sound of music wafted from the house. Marilee was playing the piano. The piece was unfamiliar but it wrapped around him like satin ribbons—or maybe a woman's loving arms.

Startled by the image that came to mind, he stood in the dark listening until the music stopped and there was nothing more to do but go back to his own lonely abode.

Chapter 8

During the week that followed, everything worked out according to plan. On Friday, Marilee opened the door and Mo took off like a streak of lightning.

She felt a certain obligation to follow through with her part of the bargain, but there really was no way of knowing if Mo reached his destination. Unless, of course, she drove into town to check.

Telling herself that she had only the most noble of motives in mind, she harnessed her horse to the wagon the moment Timmy's lesson was over.

Mo barked in greeting as she walked into the blacksmith shop. Jed looked up from his workbench, and she was momentarily distracted by the blue depth of his eyes.

Catching herself staring, she pulled her gaze away to pet Mo. "I—I just wanted to make sure he got here okay," she stammered, feeling foolish. She shouldn't have come.

Jed wiped his hands on a rag. "Just as we planned," he said and smiled.

She smiled, too. "I—I won't keep you then." She glanced at his workbench.

He followed her gaze to the haphazard accumulation of motor parts and tools. "Thank you for taking care of him."

"It was my pleasure," she said. Mission accomplished, she turned and walked out of the shop, the hem of her skirt flapping against her ankles.

On Sunday, Jed sat next to Maizie in church, and Marilee didn't get a chance to talk to him and find out how Mo was faring.

Late that Monday afternoon, Mo showed up on her doorstep. As usual, the dog smelled like he was pickled in tuna, and his fur was matted with dirt. A good scrubbing took care of both problems in quick order. She towel-dried him and brushed him till his fur was soft and shiny, and then she changed into her prettiest blue frock.

A knock came at the door. Pinching her cheeks and moistening her lips, she hastened to answer it. It was Jed, just as she'd hoped.

"Wanted to make sure Dyna got here all right," he said, pulling off his hat and holding it to his chest. He looked particularly handsome this day. He'd gotten a haircut, and his shirt and trousers were clean and pressed, and boots polished to a high shine. Obviously, he was on his way someplace special.

"Yes, Mo got here with no trouble."

"That's good," he said. They stood staring at each other. "Something sure does smell good," he said.

"Roast beef." She hesitated. "I'd invite you to stay, but I know you have other plans."

He looked puzzled. "I don't have any plans, except to go home."

"Oh, I thought. . ." She glanced at his shiny boots. "Then perhaps you would care to join me for supper? There's plenty." She'd made certain of that.

He stood on the walkway in front of her house, a crescent-moon grin on his face. "Well now. Since you put it that way. . ."

The following Monday when Jed showed up on her doorstep to check that Mo had safely arrived at her house, he stayed for both supper and a piano lesson.

They sat side by side on the piano bench, elbows and shoulders touching, and she took him through the basics. He was a fast learner and seemed to enjoy the lesson. Mo enjoyed it, too. Not once did the dog growl or bark, not even when Jed hit a wrong note.

Jed didn't have a piano to practice on, so Marilee invited him to come back the following night. Taking her up on the offer, he appeared on her doorstep with a huge bouquet of sunflowers, a bone for Mo, and a candy dish to replace the one he'd broken.

On Wednesday night he showed up with a bowl of fresh strawberries from his aunt's garden, a piece of rawhide for Mo, and a tool kit to fix the broken leg on the chair he'd sat on.

On Thursday he surprised her with a box of striped candy—her favorite—a rubber ball for Mo, and a new lamp to replace the one he'd knocked over the last time he came.

"You don't have to bring me gifts," she said, though secretly she was flattered.

"You won't let me pay for my piano lessons," he said. "This is the least I can do."

Mo barked in agreement, and she and Jed shared a laugh.

The Tuesday Afternoon Club met in the social hall of the Bee Flat Congregational Church. A dozen women belonged to the group, including the perpetually heartbroken Maizie Denton.

Only today she didn't look all that forlorn. For once she was all smiles as she took her place next to Marilee.

Mrs. Pickwick called the meeting to order. "Ladies," she said. "I have some exciting news. The best. . .Maizie, do you want to tell it or should I?"

Maizie grinned like a new bride. "You can tell," she said with a giggle, her curls bouncing off her shoulders. Dressed all in yellow, she looked and sounded like a canary.

"Very well," Mrs. Pickwick said. "Maizie and Jed Colbert are back together."

Marilee's mouth fell open. Jed was at her house every night for the last two weeks and hadn't said a word about Maizie. Not once during all that time had he so much as mentioned her name.

Applause followed the announcement and Marilee clapped along with everyone else, but her heart wasn't in it. Not that she wasn't happy for Maizie. Jed, too. But she would miss the long leisurely evenings she and Jed spent together. The lessons. The laughs.

"When's the wedding?" Mrs. Harper asked, and the question was like a knife in Marilee's heart.

"We haven't talked about that yet," Maizie said. "But he's taking me to the Dog Days of Summer dance on Saturday. Who knows? Maybe he'll propose to me then."

Mrs. Pickwick pressed her hand against her forehead. "Speaking of the dance, that reminds me." Her gaze shot to Marilee. "Reverend Hampton asked if you would play that night. Our usual fiddle player will be out of town."

"Well, I—"

"Oh, please say yes," Mrs. Thompson pleaded. A recent newlywed, she was a pretty soft-spoken woman with a slight lisp. "I've heard you're a talented pianist."

Mrs. Pickwick interpreted Marilee's silence as consent. "Ah, good. It's settled then."

It was far from settled, but there really was no polite way to decline.

Maizie leaned sideways. "I bet you'll be glad when the

dog situation is resolved."

"Resolved?" Marilee raised an eyebrow. "What do you mean?"

"Once I make a proper home for Jed, I'm sure Dyna won't want to wander anymore."

"I'm sure you're right," Marilee said, and added beneath her breath, "But Mo will."

That night Jed knocked on her door just like always. He looked and acted as if nothing had changed. He held flowers and candy but for once no replacements for broken furniture or knickknacks. That's because she had been quietly packing stuff away to make room for his large physique and broad movements.

"Well, aren't you going to invite me in?" he asked.

She stared at him dumbfounded. "How—how could you?"

He frowned. "How could I what?"

His innocent act floored her. More than that infuriated her.

Since he continued to stare at her as if she'd taken leave of her senses, she decided to spell it out. "I'm sure Maizie would not approve."

A baffled look crossed his face. "Why would she mind? She understands the situation."

Marilee blinked. Was that all she was? A situation. "Maybe *she* does. But *I* don't. Good night!"

With that she slammed the door in his startled face. The nerve of him! What kind of woman did he think she was? Entertaining a single man in her home was shocking enough, but bucking convention with a betrothed man went against all common decency.

Jed pounded on the door. "Marilee, open up!"

"Go away."

"We need to talk."

"We're done talking, Jed Colbert. Now leave me alone!"

Maybe it was her tone of voice. Or maybe he just got tired of standing on the doorstep, but he finally left. She moved a curtain aside and watched through the window as he rode away on his horse.

Flopping down on the sofa she squeezed her hands tight on her lap, determined to hold her emotions in check. She wasn't even aware that Mo had joined her on the sofa until he laid his head on her lap. The dog was not allowed on the furniture, but Marilee no longer cared. Nothing mattered anymore. Not her music and certainly not the blasted sofa.

And that's when the tears came.

Chapter 9

The Dog Days of Summer dance was held each year on the second Saturday in August.

Marilee crossed the still empty dance floor and sat on the bench in front of the piano. Fortunately the instrument stood next to the window and a slight breeze cooled her heated brow. The dog days of summer traditionally lasted for forty days, and she hoped that held true for this year. So far it had been a hot and sultry summer, and she was anxious for it to end.

After smoothing her blue satin skirt and adjusting the sleeves of her white lace shirtwaist, she rubbed her hands together and stretched her fingers. She then played an arpeggio to test the keys.

The piano was so old that the F sharp sounded more like a G. If that wasn't bad enough, the foot pedals groaned beneath her feet like an arthritic old man.

Nevertheless, she sat primly upon the mahogany piano

stool and gamely coached with nimble fingers whatever melody the yellowed ivories were willing to release.

Chatter mingled with the music as couples began arriving. Matronly chaperones sat on either side of the dance floor determined to nip an inappropriate touch or whispered proposition in the bud. Soon the party was in full swing.

Somberly dressed men whirled their partners around the dance floor. Next to the dark trousers and plain shirts, the women's frocks looked as bright and colorful as flowers in a summer garden.

Jed and Maizie walked in, and Marilee felt a squeezing pain in her chest. She didn't mean to stare, and when he looked her way, her fingers fumbled and she hit several wrong notes. Mortified, she pulled her gaze away from the couple and focused on the sheet of music with unseeing eyes.

Irritated at the way Jed affected her, she brought her hands down hard on the keys. Jed meant nothing to her. They were at the most friends—and new ones at that. She had no right to feel—what?

Abandoned? Betrayed? They shared a few meals together, had a few laughs. Oh, yes, and they owned the same dog. But that was no reason to feel like she'd lost something dear and precious—like pieces of her heart.

Maybe she was just lonely. She'd made friends galore since arriving in town but none were really close. Only

Jed. She'd confided in him, told him why she'd left Boston. Trusted him. Funny how two people can hit it off right away and others took a lifetime to know.

That was behind her now. She did what had to be done, and no matter how many times he'd returned to her doorstep—and there were many—she hadn't wavered.

Setting her thoughts aside, she pounded out waltzes, polkas and, for the older folks, quadrilles. Music. That's the only thing she could rely on. That and her dear heavenly Father. As for the hurt, eventually she'd get over it. She always did.

Jed knew the instant that Marilee left the dance hall. It wasn't just that the music had stopped, but the room had grown notably dimmer, as if she'd taken some of the light with her.

Fortunately, Maizie was busy talking to the new doctor in town, so she didn't notice him slip away. He hadn't even wanted to go to the dance, but Maizie had insisted "for old time's sake." By the time he realized he had feelings for Marilee, it was too late to back out.

Outside it was a warm and balmy night. A shiny gold moon glittered against a velvet jewel box sky. He found Marilee at the rear of the dance hall gazing upward.

The laughter of partygoers filtered through the slatted sides of the building, but not loud enough to drown out his pounding heart. Most certainly it was wrong of him to follow her. She obviously wanted to be alone, and she had made it clear—more than clear—that she wanted nothing more to do with him.

Still, he couldn't help himself. He wanted—needed—an explanation as to why she had suddenly turned against him. Was that too much to ask?

He hadn't known how much the evenings spent together had meant until they were no more.

He cleared his throat. "That's Sirius, the dog star," he said. "It's the brightest star in the sky." When she failed to respond he continued. "Since it was so bright, the ancients thought it contributed to the heat of the day. That's where the term 'the dog days of summer' originated."

This time she looked at him and he promptly forgot all about the night sky. Instead he wondered how her dewy lips would taste. What her hair would look like flowing down her back. How it would feel to take her in his arms and twirl her around the dance floor.

"Where's Maizie?" she asked.

He leaned against the trunk of a tree and hung his thumbs from his belt.

"Inside talking to friends."

"I better go back in." She started to leave, but he stopped her with a hand to her wrist. "Wait."

Her eyes widened and her lips parted slightly.

He forced himself to speak. "About Maizie—"

She shook her head. "Don't try to explain."

"She means nothing to me."

"Don't," she whispered. "Please don't."

Desperate to reach her, he tried another tactic. "Dyna arrived home all right." It's not what he'd wanted to say, but obviously it's what she wanted to hear for she relaxed beneath his touch. "Tomorrow I'm taking him fishing."

"I'm sure Mo will like that," she said, and the slightest smile touched the corners of her mouth.

"I miss you," he said.

The smile died, and a look of panic took its place. She pulled her hand from his and backed away. "Don't say that!"

He took a step forward. "Why not? It's true."

He heard her intake of breath. "I—I better go back inside."

He nodded but then something strange happened. It was as if his hands had a mind of their own. For suddenly he reached out and pulled her into his arms. Before either of them had a chance to recover, his lips claimed hers. And, just like that, she kissed him back.

Holy mackerel. It felt like he was floating on a cloud. Jumping Jupiter. The kiss was every bit as wondrous as he'd imagined—every bit as sweet and gentle. Every bit as tender and warm.

All too soon it ended. With a look of dismay she pushed him away. That's when the full impact of what he'd done hit him.

"I'm sorry. I had no right—"

"Go," she whispered. "Just go!"

He spun around and stopped in his tracks. Maizie stood a short distance away. Judging by the look on her face, she'd been there awhile. Eyes rounded, she let out an ear-piercing scream—just before attacking him with pounding fists.

Chapter 10

Marilee didn't dare show her face at church on Sunday. Ashamed by what had happened, she was even afraid to step foot out of the house. The gossip mongers were probably having a field day. It was like living through the Boston scandal all over again.

Why, oh, why did she let Jed kiss her? What made matters worse, she had kissed him back. Of all the stupid things to do. But all she could think about at the time were the delicious sensations his lips unleashed. His kiss had touched a part of her that only music had been able to reach. Nothing—not even the thought of playing in a full symphony orchestra—had made her feel the way Jed made her feel.

She clutched her hands together and closed her eyes. "God, forgive me. But if I had it to do all over again I would still kiss him back."

On Monday Mo returned just like he always did. He barked and scratched and barked some more, wanting to be let in.

Marilee pressed her head against the door but didn't open it. "Go away, Mo. Go home."

Having Mo under her roof was just too painful. He only reminded her of Jed and how much she missed him.

She should never have gotten involved with him. Mrs. Pickwick had warned her about his womanizing ways. But did she listen? No, she didn't! The nerve of him, using her to cheat on poor Maizie.

She palmed her forehead. Now her name was mud. Already she'd lost several students because of one unguarded moment of ecstasy.

Mo whined and barked and scratched some more, but then all was quiet. She cracked the door open. Mo was nowhere to be seen.

Closing the door, she leaned against it before sliding to the floor and promptly bursting into tears.

Curly shook his head and leaned against the door frame of the blacksmith shop. "Tell me again how you happened to take one woman to the dance and ended up kissing another."

"I'm not really sure myself," Jed said. He wasn't proud of

what he'd done. He had no right to even think about another woman until the issue with Maizie had been resolved. He thought it *had* been resolved.

Curly's forehead crumbled. "I never thought you could hurt Maizie like that."

"I didn't mean to." Jed raked his fingers through his hair. When did things get so out of control? "It was the last thing I wanted. I told her plain out that the two of us had no future together. The only reason I took her to the dance was for old time's sake. That's what she called it. How was I to know she told everyone we were a couple again, hoping that would make me change my mind?"

Curly rolled his eyes. "Sounds like you have no better luck handling women than you do your dog."

"Yeah, well, don't forget it was Dyna who got me into this mess in the first place."

"One thing is obvious," Curly said. "You have it bad for the piano teacher."

Curly didn't tell him anything he didn't already know. "Yes, but it would never work out," he said, though it pained him to admit it. "Marriage would be a disaster." He pointed to the pile of tools on his workbench. "I'm a slob. I like to go fishing and hunting and. . ." He shook his head. "I can't even sit on her furniture without causing mayhem. And her bed. . ."

Curly's eyebrows shot up and would have reached his hairline if he had one. "What about her bed?"

"She won't even let Dyna on it. What chance would I have?"

"It seems to me that you're concentrating too much on your differences and not enough on your similarities."

"What similarities? What are you talking about?"

"You both like music."

Jed shook his head. "I'm not even in the same country as she is, music-wise." He'd never even heard of Mozart and Chopping—or whatever his name was—before he met her.

Ignoring the comment, Curly continued. "You share the same dog, and most important of all, you're both Christians. Sounds like the perfect match to me."

"Try telling that to Marilee. She won't even talk to me. Said she refused to be a party to breaking Maizie's heart."

Curly shook his head. "You sure are in the doghouse."

Jed blew out his breath. He was in the doghouse all right, in more ways than one. Already he'd noticed a drop in business because of what happened at the dance. Since Marilee was part owner of the dog, he hadn't felt right about claiming the reward money. But the way things were going, he might have to collect it just to stay afloat.

A knock sounded on Marilee's door early that Saturday morning. Upon finding Jed on her doorstep, she tried closing the door but he jammed his foot in the threshold.

"I have nothing to say to you," she said through the crack.

"I just want to know if there's a problem with Dyna."

She frowned. "What do you mean?"

"He didn't show up at the shop yesterday."

She yanked the door open all the way. "Yesterday? He should have returned home on Monday."

Jed's eyes widened. "What?"

"I sent him home on Monday." She covered her mouth with her hand. "Oh, no! You don't suppose—"

He stepped inside the house. "Let's not jump to conclusions."

"But what if he's injured?" She clutched her hands to her chest. "Or was run over by a wagon. What if—"

"We'll find him," he said. "Someone must have seen him."

She gazed up at him, her eyes burning. "It's all my fault."

"It's nobody's fault," he said, his voice low. He wrapped an arm around her and murmured in her hair. "Dyna has a mind of his own. You know that."

She ducked from beneath his arm. His very nearness confused her, and right now all she could think about was Mo. *Oh, God, please let him be all right.*

Jed shuffled his feet, tugged his hat down low, and almost knocked over the lamp again. "I'll go find him."

"Wait." She grabbed her gloves and hat. "I'm going with you."

Chapter 11

Jed drove the horse and wagon up and down the streets of Bee Flat with Marilee by his side.

"Mo!" she called, cupping her hands around her mouth.

"Dyna," he shouted.

He drove clear out to the Webber farm to the west and the Anderson flour mill to the east. They rode past fields of newly harvested wheat and acres of mile-high corn. Sunflowers grew in wild abundance alongside the road, the dark bonneted faces turned toward the sun. Sheep grazed next to a woolen mill, and cows lounged beneath a grove of cottonwood trees.

Neither of them mentioned Maizie or the dance. Today was about finding their dog.

No one had seen either Mo or Dyna and, as the day wore on, Marilee grew more distraught. Jed reached over to squeeze her hand.

"We better get something to eat," he said. Already the

sun was playing footsies with the horizon, and neither of them had had a bite since morning.

She moistened her lips and nodded before pulling her hand away. A squeezing pain filled his chest as he drove back to town.

They stopped at Aunt Lula's Café, but neither he nor Marilee felt much like eating. Since it was too dark to continue the search, he drove her home and walked her to her front porch.

In the soft glow of moonlight, she looked even more beautiful than usual. "Better get some sleep," he said, his voice husky.

"You, too."

He lifted his hand to her cheek, and her skin felt cool beneath his touch. "Marilee—"

She backed away, warding him off with a shake of her head. "You'd best go."

Jed had unharnessed his horse from the wagon and started toward the wooden staircase in back of his shop leading up to his living quarters when he heard a familiar bark.

Heart leaping with joy, he spun around just as Dyna came shooting out of the dark. The dog jumped up on him, tail wagging so hard his entire body swayed from side to side.

Jed ran his hands through the dog's fur. "Where you been, boy, eh? I've searched high and low for you."

"He's been with me."

Jed lifted his gaze just as Curly stepped out of the shadows and into the yellow haze of the street lamp.

"Where'd you find him?"

"I didn't. He found me."

Jed straightened. "What's that supposed to mean?"

"He showed up on my doorstep last Monday."

"Monday!" Jed pushed Dyna down. "You had him all this time and never said a word?" He stared at his friend, incredulous. "You knew Marilee and I would be out of our minds with worry. What were you thinking?"

Instead of looking apologetic or regretful, Curly shrugged. "Don't blame me. Blame Dyna. He's a cow dog. He has herding instincts."

Jed's temper snapped. "What's that supposed to mean?"

"Bringin' critters together is what he does best, and I'd say he's done a good job of bringin' you and that pretty music teacher together. If you didn't take advantage of his disappearin' act then you're a bigger fool than I thought."

"What are you talking about? Take advantage. Why would I do such a thing?"

"Because that fella with a bow and arrow sure buggered you up. I mean we're talking big time."

Jed opened his mouth but denial stuck in his throat. "I don't want to hear this." He didn't need Curly or anyone else telling him what he already knew. He took the stairs two at a time with Dyna at his heel. He opened the door to his place and struck a match to light the lamp.

Curly walked in uninvited. "You might not want to hear it, but it's true. I can see it in your face. Nothin' makes a man look more miserable than love."

Jed wasn't sure that's how he looked, but it sure in blazes was how he felt. "It doesn't matter. It would never work out."

"You keep saying that."

"That's because it's true. She has a whole lot of book learning. Me? I didn't even finish sixth grade."

"So? Stay away from topics that require five-dollar words."

Jed grimaced. Vocabulary was the least of his problems. "Do you know who she was engaged to marry, back in Boston? A US Senator." God knows, even her scandals were high class. Most scandals involved money or sex, but not Marilee's; hers concerned no less than a symphony orchestra and a member of congress.

Curly shrugged. "She didn't marry him, did she?"

"No, but she would have had he not lost the election."

"If that's what's bothering you, then run for office. I hear tell that they're looking for someone to run for dogcatcher— too many dogs running around loose," he said with a pointed look at Dyna. "You'd be a shoo-in."

"I'm not running for dogcatcher."

"Well, you gotta do something. Otherwise you're gonna lose her fur good."

Jed sighed. "I've already lost her for good. She made it perfectly clear that she did not want to hurt Maizie more than she already was."

Curly made a divisive sound with his mouth. "You can forget about Maizie. After the fiasco at the dance, the new doctor took her home, and they've been cozying up ever since."

Jed's eyebrows rose. "Are you saying that Maizie and the doctor—?"

"Yep. It sure didn't take her long to get over you, did it? What is it they say about out of sight out of—?"

Jed's mind whirled. With Maizie out of the picture, he was free to. . .what? Mope around? Follow his heart? Continue his lonely life? The last thought moved him across the room. "Stop yakking and help me with this." Jed scooted the well-worn couch away from the wall.

Curly frowned, but he grabbed hold of the other side of the couch. "Why in tarnation are we moving furniture? And watch my back—"

"Quit complaining. You told me to do something and that's what I'm doing."

Early Monday morning, a rap sounded at Marilee's door. She glanced at the tall clock. Normally this was time for Lucy Dillon's piano lesson, but her parents fired Marilee following the Dog Days of Summer dance scandal.

She opened the door and blinked. Was that a couch? On her front lawn? She leaned forward for a closer look. It was a couch all right, but what was that awful piece of junk doing there?

She stepped onto the porch. Seeing Jed, she froze, as did her heart. "What is the meaning of this?" she managed to squeak out. "Why is this. . .this thing in front of my house?"

"This. . ." Jed began, "is a solid piece of furniture." He plopped on it and bounced up and down. "A man can sit on it without fearing for his life. Best of all, it will hold two people and even a dog all at the same time."

"Mo?" she whispered.

He slanted a nod toward the horse and wagon parked in front of her house.

She craned her neck for a better view, and her heart leaped with joy. "You found him!"

"Actually, he found me."

Her hands flew to her chest. "Thank God!" Drawing her gaze back to Jed she frowned. "But that still doesn't explain what this sofa is doing in my front yard."

"Oh, this." He rubbed the back of his neck and gave her a sheepish look. "I have something important to say. When I talk I tend to need a lot of elbow room, and if I have to replace any more broken stuff I'll end up in the poorhouse." He patted a sagging cushion. "I was hoping that the second person it would hold would be you."

Her breath caught in her lungs. Why was he doing this to her? "I told you I can't." She swallowed hard. "Maizie—"

He shook his head. "I just came away from seeing Maizie. She's now being courted by the new doctor and gave us her blessing." He waited for her to say something, and when she didn't he added, "Maizie has known for weeks that it was over between her and me. She just didn't want to believe it."

Marilee didn't move; she couldn't, for fear of waking up and discovering that none of this was real.

"No matter what you might have heard, I don't lie, and I don't cheat. I also have no right to be here." A muscle quivered at his jaw as he continued. "I don't have much school learning, and I'm never gonna run for dogcatcher. I'll probably tramp dirt on your rugs and forget to use a napkin. There'll also be times I'll come home smelling like a kettle of fish, and we'll probably have to keep replacing lamps." He drew his eyebrows together. "I'm not doing a very good job of selling myself, am I?"

"You're. . .you're doing just fine," she whispered.

Eyes burning with intensity, he continued. "What I'm trying to say is that I love you. Don't know how those Chopping or Bay-toven fellows would have said it. All I can tell you is that I love you to the Dog Star and back."

She stared at him, unable to find her voice. Did he say love?

He rubbed his chin. "Do. . . Do you think you can make room in your life for a big oaf like me?"

Her heart pounded, and she inhaled sharply. She'd avoided naming her feelings for Jed for fear it would only lead to another broken dream. But now the word *love* played across her heartstrings and reached into the deepest part of her soul. The music rose to such a crescendo that she had to run to keep up with the rhythm.

And run she did, down the porch steps and into his arms. "Oh, Jed!" He fell back with a startled look, but that didn't keep him from pulling her close and showering her with kisses. Or maybe she was the one showering him.

"I love you," she said when they stopped for air. "I love you more than Chopin and Schubert and Beethoven and—"

Jed matched her declarations with a few of his own—all to the tune of Mo's incessant barks.

Reluctantly, Marilee pulled her mouth away from his. "Do you think Mo planned for us to be together?" she asked. It sounded crazy, but after everything that happened, not that implausible.

Jed thought for a moment before shaking his head. "He might have brought us together, but I'd say that God was pulling the whiskers."

She laughed. "The *God* days of summer," she murmured between kisses.

She then drew her head back and called, "Come on, Mo." The dog barked but remained in the wagon.

Jed whistled. "Dyna! Come on, boy." Still the dog refused to budge.

She met Jed's gaze. "What do you suppose is wrong? Why won't he come?"

"I don't know. Unless. . ." Jed lifted his voice. "Dyna-Mo. Come."

This time the dog jumped out of the wagon, cut across

the yard, and jumped on the couch, all wagging tail and slobbering tongue.

Jed laughed. "So what do you say? Will you take this sorrowful looking piece of furniture to be your lawfully wedded couch?"

She pretended to give the matter some thought. "Only if you and Dyna-Mo come with it."

Jed turned to their dog. "What do you say, boy? Is it a deal?"

Awf.

Jed grinned. "You heard it from the boss."

Joy bubbled out of her as she pulled from his arms. She then grabbed his hand and coaxed him to his feet. Laughing like a schoolgirl, she led him up the porch and into the house with Dyna-Mo at their heels.

"What are we doing?" Jed asked, knocking against the lamp.

Releasing his hand, she moved to the side of her sofa and pointed to the other end. "Grab hold," she said. "We're moving this one out and the other one in." The stilted furnishings were better suited for Boston's formal lifestyle and not for the new life ahead of her as Mrs. Jed Colbert.

Jed grinned from ear to ear. "Well, now. I'd say that's a doggone good idea. What do you say, boy?"

For answer Dyna-Mo wagged his tail and flopped down on the floor as if he meant to stay.

Bestselling author Margaret Brownley has penned more than thirty novels. Her books have won numerous awards, including Readers' Choice and Award of Excellence. She's a former Romance Writers of America RITA finalist and has written for a TV soap. Happily married to her real-life hero, Margaret and her husband have three grown children and live in Southern California. Visit her at www.margaret-brownley.com

THE FOURTH OF JULY BRIDE

by Amanda Cabot

Chapter 1

Cheyenne, Wyoming Territory
June 1, 1886

I'm sorry, Miss Towson. I know you'd hoped for a different outcome. So did I."

Though Dr. Winston was discussing her mother, he directed his comments to Naomi as he said, "Your mother's condition is deteriorating more quickly than I had hoped. I imagine you've noticed that."

Naomi nodded. No one could deny that Ma had been bumping into more things recently. The new spectacles that had cost far too much didn't seem to be making any difference, and the brown eyes that had once been the same shade as Naomi's seemed cloudier each day.

"How long do we have?" she asked. Ma was being uncharacteristically reticent and had said nothing since the doctor had completed his examination.

Doc's frown seemed at odds with his boyish face. Though many in the city believed him too young to be capable,

Naomi had as much confidence in him as she did in Gideon Carlisle's ability to raise the best cattle in the territory. She shook herself mentally. Now was not the time to be thinking about Gideon.

"I hope I'm wrong," the doctor said, "but if the disease continues to progress at its current rate, your mother will be totally blind before Christmas."

Christmas! Naomi gripped the edge of the battered desk, struggling not to cry out. Every other time she'd brought her mother here, she'd found reassurance in the slightly shabby office. Not today. If Doc Winston was right, she and Ma had less than seven months before their lives reached another crossroads.

Naomi had believed they had far longer than that. It was true that Ma's eyesight had failed so much that she'd been unable to sew since last November, leaving Naomi as the family's sole support, but neither of them had expected total darkness to be so close.

As Ma nodded in apparent resignation, Naomi wrapped an arm around her shoulders. Her mother might have accepted her future, but she had not.

"Isn't there something we can do? Stronger spectacles? Different eye drops?" Though Naomi hated sounding desperate, she couldn't bear the thought that the woman who looked far younger than her forty-five years might lose what little vision remained. Naomi would do anything she could to save her mother's sight, and if that involved another pair of spectacles, somehow she'd find the money to pay for them.

The doctor shook his head. "Neither spectacles nor eyedrops will slow or stop the disease. There's only one possibility, and it's risky."

For the first time since they'd entered the office, Ma straightened her spine and looked directly at the physician. "Tell us more," she said, her voice as determined as ever.

Doc leaned across his desk, his expression radiating excitement. "I've read about surgery to remove the growths. If it's successful, patients experience a restoration of sight." His smile faded. "I must warn you, though, that there are many dangers. If infection sets in, death may occur."

The way he refused to meet her gaze when he pronounced the last sentence told Naomi he was worried. "What are the chances of that?"

"About half."

Terrible odds. Feeling her mother shudder, Naomi looked at the doctor. "Would you give us a few minutes alone?"

"Certainly."

When he left the room, Naomi turned so she was facing her mother. "What do you think?" Ma might not see clearly, but Naomi did, and she wanted to read her mother's expression.

"I don't want to be a burden to you." Ma's words were firm. "You've been the best of daughters. Not once have I heard you complain, even when you've had to shoulder more responsibility. By now you should have a husband and children of your own. Instead you're spending your life caring for me."

Naomi shook her head vehemently. It was true that she dreamed of marriage and cradling a baby in her arms, but until recently, there had been no man with whom she could picture sharing the rest of her life. And now, even though one man fired her imagination, she knew he was not the one God intended for her.

"There was no one I wanted to marry. I didn't love any of the men who came to call, not the way I love you." She gripped Ma's hand, needing the physical contact with the woman she loved so dearly. "The surgery frightens me, but it's your decision. I want to do whatever will make you happiest."

Her mother was silent for a moment, her eyes focusing on something in the distance. Then she spoke with no hesitation. "I don't want to be blind. I'm not afraid to face death, but I am a coward where blindness is concerned."

"Then we'll have the surgery." Naomi rose and opened the door, welcoming the doctor back to his office. "We've made our decision," she told him.

"It's a wise choice," he said when Naomi explained her mother's wishes. "I'd like to do it immediately, but that's not possible. I want to have a more experienced physician assist me." He pulled out a telegram. "Dr. Hibbard is the best in the country. I took the liberty of consulting him.

He's willing to come out here, but he's not available until the middle of September."

"I can wait." Though they were only three short words, Naomi heard the enthusiasm in her mother's voice. After months of steadily declining vision, Ma finally had a reason to hope.

"There's one other thing," Doc said, "and that's Dr. Hibbard's fee."

Naomi tried not to flinch. Somehow she'd find the money. Perhaps Esther would let her work more hours. But when Doc named the amount, Naomi felt as if she were drowning and someone had just pulled the life preserver away from her. The other doctor's fee was more than she could earn in a year.

"So much?" Ma's voice rose with disbelief.

"He's the best," Doc explained, "and he's agreed to travel all the way from Boston to help you."

"I see." But the truth was, Naomi didn't see how she'd be able to pay for the operation her mother so desperately needed.

As if he understood her dilemma, Doc steepled his fingers and nodded. "You don't need to make the decision today. I told my colleague I'd have an answer for him next week."

"Thank you for everything you've done, Doc. I won't mislead you. It'll take a miracle to find that much money." Naomi rose and helped her mother to her feet. "Let's go home, Ma. It's time to pray for a miracle."

He missed her. Gideon Carlisle tried not to frown. That would only make things more difficult for the artist, and that was not Gideon's intention. Jeremy Snyder had rearranged his schedule and was working extra hours to accommodate Gideon. The least Gideon could do was keep a pleasant expression on his face while his portrait was being painted. But he couldn't deny that he missed Naomi.

Though her beauty had caught his eye the first time he'd come here, he'd soon discovered there was much more to Naomi Towson than glossy brown hair, eyes the color of chocolate, and perfect features. Her wit and sense of humor were the reason he looked forward to his portrait sessions. Of course, he wouldn't tell Jeremy that.

"When can I see what you've done?" Gideon asked, trying to keep his thoughts from the lovely young woman who should be standing behind the counter helping customers decide whether to buy white or pumpernickel.

Though a bakery was an unusual place for an artist's studio, no one in Cheyenne seemed to care that Jeremy Snyder painted in a corner of his wife's bakery rather than in a studio of his own. His talent had made him one of the city's premier artists, and that was all that mattered.

Jeremy nodded as if he'd expected the question. "Another week. I promised it would be finished by June 10, and it will be. Don't worry, Gideon. Your mother will have it before the Fourth of July."

"Thanks." Gideon realized he'd never told Jeremy the reason he had commissioned his portrait at this particular time. "Mother's been pestering me to go back East to celebrate our nation's birthday ever since I arrived here. For some reason she won't believe me when I tell her Cheyenne has its own celebration and that it's a fine one. The painting is my attempt to placate her. I figured if she couldn't have me, she could have my likeness."

As he mixed paints on his palette, Jeremy nodded again. "If she's like many of the women I know, she'll want her friends to see both her son's likeness and the house he's built." It had been Jeremy's suggestion to include Gideon's home as part of the background, and he'd spent hours sketching the three-story mansion on what was being called Millionaires' Row.

Gideon still marveled at how he'd parlayed a small investment and a lot of hard work into a sizable fortune. There was no doubt about it. The grasslands of eastern Wyoming were the ideal spot to raise cattle. His had thrived to the point where he was now considered a cattle baron.

Gideon wrinkled his nose. He wasn't certain he liked that term, but he did like knowing that his mother could no longer claim that he was wasting his life. As the oldest of four sons, Gideon had been expected to follow his father's example and join the family law firm, but the law had never appealed to him. For as long as Gideon could recall, he'd wanted to spend his days outside. And now he did.

"Would you like some coffee and a piece of cake?" Esther Snyder asked as she approached her husband's studio. Though it consisted of nothing more than two stools and space for Jeremy's easel, the studio's location next to the tables where customers enjoyed cakes and cookies gave them the opportunity to see an artist working and had led to both additional commissions for Jeremy and more sales for Esther.

Esther laid the tray on the closest table and removed two plates of cake and a pair of coffee mugs. "It looks like Jeremy's ready for a break, and I suspect you are, too."

It was true that Gideon looked forward to the breaks, but the reason had little to do with the food. It was Naomi's company that made them special. "Did Naomi make the cake?" Perhaps she was merely running errands for Esther and would soon return. Though decorum dictated that he not mention her increasing girth, Gideon knew that Esther and Jeremy were expecting their first child before summer ended and that Naomi had been hired so that Esther could rest occasionally.

Esther shook her head. "Not today. She had to take her mother to the doctor this morning and asked for the whole day off." Esther gave Gideon an appraising look, as if she realized his question had been more than casual. "She'll be back tomorrow."

"Good." He wouldn't insult Esther by telling her that

Naomi was a better baker. It might not even be true. After all, it was possible that the stories Naomi told while she shared cake and coffee with him were what made the baked goods taste so delicious. All Gideon knew was that he had no appetite this afternoon.

He rose and stretched, then looked at Jeremy, who had wrapped his brush in a cloth. "If you're finished with me today, I've got some business to attend to." It wasn't a lie, but the simple truth was that Gideon wanted to be anywhere but here where Naomi's absence weighed on him.

Once outside, he headed north to Twentieth Street, then walked two blocks west to Ferguson. He'd built his house on the corner next to Barrett Landry, the man some said would be one of Wyoming's first senators once the territory gained statehood. Gideon didn't care about that today. Today he didn't care about much, and that wasn't normal. Ever since he'd discovered Naomi wasn't at the bakery, Gideon had been disgruntled. Surely that would improve once he was home.

"Good afternoon, sir," Preble said as he opened the door. In his midforties, Preble was tall, thin, and distinguished, the perfect butler. "I put the mail in your office."

The small frown that accompanied his statement made Gideon ask if anything was wrong.

"I'm not certain, sir. You have a letter from Mrs. Carlisle."

No wonder Preble was concerned. Gideon's mother

was as reliable as the Union Pacific, writing one letter each week, and that letter always arrived on Friday. Today was Tuesday.

Gideon nodded and handed his hat to Preble. "I'd better see what she has to say." Seconds later, he stood behind his desk and slid the single sheet of paper from the envelope. His eyes widened as he read the few words she'd inscribed. No! Not that!

Chapter 2

Gideon stared at the paper, unable to believe the words now engraved on his brain.

"Bad news, sir?" Preble stood stiffly in the doorway. Even though Gideon had told him there was no need for formality when they were alone, Preble had firm ideas of a butler's role and was not inclined to bend them.

"I suppose that depends on your definition," Gideon said. "My mother is planning to pay me a visit. It appears she doesn't believe my tales of Cheyenne's Independence Day celebration and wants to see it for herself." When Preble nodded, Gideon continued. "She's arriving on June 18 and will be here for two weeks." Or longer, if Gideon failed to meet the condition she'd outlined.

"I don't understand, sir. That sounds like good news to me. Surely she will be impressed with the city."

"If only that were all." Though Preble was privy to most of Gideon's business dealings, he would not tell his trusted butler some things, including his mother's determination to see him married.

It's time for you to wed, Gideon. If you can't find a bride in Cheyenne, I'll order one for you. Gladys Fowler's son sent for one by mail, and she's already a grandmother three times over.

"My mother is a stubborn woman. Once she makes up her mind, there's no way to change it." As distasteful as the prospect was, Mother would be here in less than three weeks, fully intending to set her last living son on the road to matrimony.

Preble inclined his head slightly. "I can assure you the house will be spotless and the meals excellent."

"I hope that will be enough." But it wouldn't. The sole thing that would satisfy Mother would be a bride or at least a fiancée.

There had to be a way out of this predicament, Gideon told himself as he paced the floor, ignoring the pot of coffee and plate of sandwiches Preble had brought him. Mother might be stubborn, but so was Gideon. No matter what she said, no matter what she threatened, he would not marry simply because she believed it was time. There had to be another way.

"What's wrong, dear?" Esther asked as she measured a spoonful of peppermint leaves into the teapot. Though the bakery's owner was normally in the kitchen hours before Naomi, today she'd gone to Fort Russell to visit her niece and had left Naomi in charge. Within minutes of her return, Esther had turned her attention from the cakes Naomi had made to Naomi herself.

"Nothing's wrong." It was a lie, but Naomi didn't want to distress the woman who'd been so kind to her. Not only had Esther given her a job when she needed one, but she'd become more friend than employer, sharing both her kitchen and her clothes with Naomi until Naomi had saved enough to buy the simple skirts and waists that Esther deemed appropriate garb for the showroom part of the bakery.

Esther shook her head again and pulled two cups and saucers from the cabinet. "Your face tells a different story." She touched her expanding waistline. "You needn't coddle me, you know. Having a baby is perfectly natural, even at my advanced age."

Though Esther's lips quirked into a wry smile, Naomi knew she worried about being too old to be having her first child. She'd confided that both she and Jeremy had believed themselves beyond the age for marriage and had felt blessed to have discovered love. Learning that Esther was with child soon after their wedding had brought them both unexpected happiness and worries. Perhaps that was the reason Esther felt the need for the soothing comfort of mint tea.

"You and Jeremy aren't old," Naomi said firmly. Jeremy was just over forty, and Esther had yet to reach that age.

"You're going to be the best parents any child would want."

"With God's help." The way Esther touched her stomach told Naomi the baby was kicking. "And with God's help and a cup of my peppermint tea, whatever is bothering you will lessen. Now, sit down, drink the tea, and tell me what's wrong."

Naomi blinked back the tears that had been so close to the surface ever since she'd heard the doctor's diagnosis, knowing she might as well tell Esther what had happened. One way or another, the older woman would get the truth from her. "It's Ma. Doc Winston says she'll be blind before Christmas unless she has surgery."

"Is she afraid of it?"

Naomi shook her head and took a sip of the steaming tea. Esther was right. Both the aroma and the flavor of the tea were soothing. Unfortunately, tea would not resolve Naomi's problem. "No. She's willing to take the risk, but we can't afford the doctor's fee."

"Don't worry." Leaning across the table, Esther put her hand on top of Naomi's, her touch as reassuring as her words. "Jeremy and I will help you."

If only it were so simple. Naomi's eyes filled with tears again as she told Esther the amount and watched the blood drain from her friend's face.

"Oh, my dear. We don't have that kind of money."

"I know. No one does." At least no one she could ask for a loan.

If rumors were true, Gideon Carlisle had more than enough money to pay for ten surgeries, but though Naomi spent half an hour with the man on the days when he came for his portrait sitting, listening to tales of his adventures as a cattle baron and sharing stories of her decidedly more prosaic life, she could not possibly ask him for money. A lady simply did not do that, no matter how kind the man appeared to be, no matter how often the lady's thoughts turned to him. Naomi couldn't ask Gideon any more than she could approach a banker for a loan, not when she had no way of repaying it.

Esther was silent for a moment, her expression so peaceful Naomi knew she was praying. Then as the sound of men's laughter drifted into the kitchen, Esther rose and put her arm around Naomi's shoulders, giving them a quick squeeze. "God will provide," she said. "He always does." Moving to the other side of the room, she pulled a tray from one of the cabinets.

"Right now you need to provide for Gideon Carlisle. I never saw the man as disgruntled as he was yesterday. I offered him spice cake, but he wouldn't eat it because you hadn't baked it."

The thought gave Naomi her first smile of the day. "That's silly. You're a better baker than I am."

"Not according to him. Now, pour his coffee and take him a piece of that chocolate cake you made with the lemon filling. You know how he likes that."

"Of course." Naomi brushed the tears from her eyes before patting her hair to ensure that no strands had come loose. It might be foolish to be primping like this, but she wanted to look her best. Gideon Carlisle wasn't simply a customer; he was... She paused, trying but failing to find the correct word. All she could say about Gideon was that he was special.

When she entered the bakery's main room, he was in his normal spot, his back to the room as he posed for Jeremy. His blond hair was as unruly as ever, the curls refusing to be subdued even by macassar oil. Though she couldn't see them, Naomi knew that his eyes were the deep blue of a summer sky and that his nose tipped ever so slightly to the right. Gideon Carlisle wasn't the most handsome man she'd ever seen, but his face was one she could not forget.

Normally he waited until she had placed the tray on the table before he moved, but today he turned at the sound of her footsteps and rose from his stool.

"I'm glad you're here," he said. Surely she only imagined the strain in Gideon's voice. He gestured to a chair. "Please sit down. I have a proposition for you."

Chapter 3

"A proposition?" Naomi couldn't imagine what Gideon meant, but this was neither the time nor the place for a serious discussion. Over the course of the weeks Gideon had been sitting for his portrait, he and Naomi had discussed many things, but with the exception of God—a subject on which they had a decided difference of opinion—they normally focused on lighter topics. Judging from Gideon's expression, this proposal—whatever it was—was serious.

As if he recognized their need for privacy, Jeremy laid down his brush and headed for the kitchen, leaving Naomi and Gideon alone in an unexpectedly empty bakery. At least now no one would overhear whatever it was Gideon planned to propose.

He took the chair on the opposite side of the table, ignoring the coffee and cake she'd laid at his place. That simple action confirmed Naomi's belief that today was not an ordinary day. Normally Gideon assuaged his thirst with a slug of coffee before he spoke.

"I find myself in a bit of a dilemma," he said. "My mother is coming to Cheyenne."

Naomi didn't bother to mask her confusion. She wasn't certain what she'd expected, but it wasn't that. "That's good, isn't it? I remember you saying you hadn't seen her since you moved here." And that had been more than three years ago. Naomi couldn't imagine going three years without talking to her mother. Letters were all fine and good, but they could not compare to hearing Ma's voice and feeling her arms around her.

Gideon started to reach for the coffee, then drew his hand back. Something must be seriously wrong if he still wasn't drinking.

"It would be fine if her only reason for coming was to visit," he said. "Unfortunately, she has another motive. Mother plans to find me a wife."

When the doorbell tinkled and a customer entered the bakery, Esther hurried out to serve her. It was an ordinary day for most of Cheyenne's residents, but clearly not for Gideon.

Faced with his astonishing statement, Naomi found herself at a loss for words. "A wife, but. . ." Though her thoughts were whirling faster than a tumbleweed in a winter wind, she couldn't form them into coherent sentences.

A small smile crossed Gideon's face. "That was my first reaction. If I didn't love my mother, I would simply tell her

I'm twenty-eight years old and the decision of who and when to marry is mine, but I can't do that. She'd be hurt. Besides, Mother's a determined woman—some would call her stubborn—and she won't give up. She really will send for a mail-order bride if I don't find one on my own."

From the first day she'd met him, one of the things Naomi had admired about Gideon was his determination. Though she'd assumed he owed that to his father, who'd been a prominent attorney in Philadelphia, now she realized that it had been inherited from his mother. Today Gideon needed more than determination. He needed a wife.

"I wish there were something I could do to help you."

His smile grew, and a twinkle filled those deep blue eyes. "There is. You can be my wife."

Naomi felt the blood drain from her face, and her heart began to pound as she stared at the man she thought she knew. Surely he hadn't said what she thought she'd heard.

He nodded as if he'd read her mind. "That's my proposition." As if pronouncing the words had returned him to his normal routine, Gideon reached for the coffee and took a sip. "I realized I don't actually need a wife. All I need is a fiancée for the two weeks Mother will be here. I'd like you to pretend to be my fiancée until the Fourth of July."

While Gideon spoke as calmly as if they were discussing the possibility of a late spring snowfall, Naomi's pulse continued to race. She heard the words, but their full meaning had yet to register. *Wife. Fiancée. Pretend.* Those simple words had never before been applied to her.

"It wouldn't demand too much of your time," Gideon continued, "though I would expect you to attend the celebrations and a few other events with Mother and me."

Naomi hadn't imagined it. He was serious. "I'm not the woman you want. Your mother will expect someone like Miriam Taggert." Not only was Miss Taggert beautiful, but as the daughter of one of Cheyenne's premier newspapermen, she frequented the same social circles as Gideon.

The corners of his mouth curved up as if he were amused. "I've met Miriam Taggert," he said. "She may have more expensive clothing than you, but she's only half the woman you are."

Gideon's compliment sent blood rushing to her cheeks. "Clothes matter," Naomi said, then laid her fingers on her lips. That sounded as if she were considering his proposal. Surely she wasn't.

"I agree. I'm also certain Madame Charlotte will be happy to create an entire wardrobe for you. At my expense, of course."

"That wouldn't be proper." A well-bred lady did not accept personal items like clothing from a man who was not her husband.

Gideon disagreed. "The rules are less stringent for affianced couples. Besides, Madame Charlotte has a reputation for discretion."

Naomi took a deep breath, trying to imagine herself in

one of the famous modiste's gowns. Though Naomi had never set foot inside the shop, she knew that Élan was where all the best dressed younger women in Cheyenne bought their clothes. She'd heard several of them complimenting each other on their exquisite gowns when they stopped at the bakery for a pastry and a cup of tea.

Gideon reached across the table and laid his hand on top of one of Naomi's. "Please say yes. I need your help." His blue eyes darkened, leaving her no doubt of his sincerity. "I'm not asking you to do this out of the goodness of your heart. I can offer you more than the clothes you'll need for this charade."

He lowered his gaze for a second, then looked at Naomi again. "I didn't mean to eavesdrop, but I couldn't help overhearing your conversation with Esther. If you'll pretend to be my fiancée, I'll pay for your mother's surgery."

Naomi's breath caught as hope surged through her. Was this the miracle she'd prayed for? It felt like it, and yet she wasn't certain. "I'd be living a lie. That would be dishonest."

Gideon shook his head. "I won't deny that there would be some deception, but no one would be hurt by it. My mother will be happy, and your mother will have a chance to have her sight restored." He squeezed Naomi's hand. "Say yes, Naomi. Please."

She was tempted. Oh, yes, she was. There was no denying the appeal of attending the opera, perhaps even dining at the InterOcean with Gideon. The clothing that he promised would be beautiful, but what attracted her most was the idea of spending more time with Gideon. Naomi enjoyed his company more than any man she'd ever met, and even when they were apart, Gideon was never far from her thoughts. Though she'd told no one, she'd dreamed of strolling through the park, her hand on his arm. If she accepted his proposal, that could happen.

Naomi closed her eyes for a second, trying to marshal her thoughts. Was Gideon right in saying that no one would be hurt? If so, she owed it to her mother to agree. Hadn't she said she'd do anything within her power to save Ma's eyesight? Besides, the pretense would last only a few weeks, for as much as Naomi enjoyed Gideon's company, she could never marry him, even if he asked her.

From early childhood on, Naomi had known that the man she married must have a strong faith. Gideon did not. Their one serious disagreement had come the day Gideon had said that he hadn't attended church services in years and had no intention of ever doing so again.

"Why should I worship a God who doesn't love me?" he'd asked, and nothing Naomi had said had changed his mind.

As the memory of Gideon's declaration echoed through her brain, an idea began to take root. Perhaps this was the miracle she'd prayed for, a way to pay for Ma's surgery, but perhaps it was more than that. Perhaps Naomi was being given the opportunity to make a difference in Gideon's life.

She nodded slowly. "All right, Gideon. I'll do it. I'll be

your pretend fiancée on one condition: I expect you to go to church with me."

Gideon strode down Seventeenth Street, scarcely glancing at the opera house and the other buildings that dominated this section of the city. He had far more important things to worry about than what Arp and Hammond had displayed in their front windows. Relief that Naomi had agreed to his plan mingled with regret. He hadn't expected her to add a stipulation to their agreement, especially not that one. For the briefest of moments, Gideon had considered rescinding his proposal, but he did not, for he knew of no other woman in Cheyenne who could play the role he needed.

Gideon had met a number of single women whose mothers considered him a good catch, but they'd bored him. Even if one of them would agree to a pretend engagement, Mother would never believe he planned to marry her. Miriam Taggert was the exception. She was intelligent and entertaining, but unless he was mistaken, Barrett Landry intended to court her. Gideon wouldn't interfere with that. Besides, Naomi was a better choice. She was fun, she was feisty, and Mother would like her. If only she hadn't insisted on attending church.

He pushed open the door to Mullen's Fine Jewelry and blinked to adjust his eyes to the relative darkness.

"It's good to see you again, Mr. Carlisle." The proprietor whose massive handlebar mustache was as famous as the quality of his merchandise greeted Gideon. "I trust your mother liked her brooch."

"She did indeed, but today I want something different. I need a ring for my fiancée." Though it felt odd saying the word, Gideon knew he had to get used to it if the charade was going to be a success.

Mr. Mullen nodded as he led the way to one of the back counters. "Do I know the lucky lady?"

"I doubt it, but she's special." Even if Sunday mornings were painful, the rest of their short betrothal would be enjoyable, because—as he'd told Mr. Mullen—Naomi was a special woman. "I want something special for her."

The jeweler reached beneath the glass and pulled out a tray of rings. Though most were diamonds in various shapes and sizes, there was also an assortment of pearls and colored stones. And, as had been the case when he'd chosen his mother's brooch, each piece was beautifully made.

"These are my finest pieces," Mr. Mullen said, "but if none of them suit you, I can make something different."

Gideon had no time for custom jewelry. He planned to slip a ring on Naomi's finger tomorrow before she had a chance to reconsider their agreement. He glanced at the tray, smiling as one caught his eye. "That's the one. It's perfect."

Ten minutes later, Gideon was headed home, the square ring box tucked inside his pocket. As he walked north on Ferguson, his pace decidedly slower than when he'd left the bakery, he paused at the corner of Eighteenth Street. It wasn't difficult to understand why this location had gained the nickname of Church Corner, since it boasted churches on three of the corners.

Looking at the buildings, he wondered which one Naomi expected him to attend. Though his muscles tensed as he clenched his fists, Gideon tried to dismiss the sinking feeling that filled him at the thought of entering the house of God. That was far more dishonest than his pretend engagement.

Gideon hadn't set foot inside a church since the day God refused to answer his prayer. How could he praise a God who let his father and three brothers die of typhoid? Gideon couldn't, and he refused to be a hypocrite by attending weekly services as if he were a true believer. But now, thanks to Naomi, he had to do exactly that. He could only hope there would be no lightning bolts when he walked through the doors.

Chapter 4

Naomi was humming as she entered the small apartment she shared with her mother. It might consist of only two rooms and a tiny kitchen, but that had always been enough for them. She had heard others speak of feeling as if a great weight had been lifted from their shoulders, but she hadn't experienced that until this afternoon. For the past year, her worries about Ma had overshadowed everything, even the beauty of spring. Now those worries were greatly reduced, all because of Gideon.

"You sound happy," Ma said, raising her cheek for a kiss as she stirred the beef stew whose delicious aroma was filling the apartment. "I haven't heard you hum in weeks."

"I am happy." Rather than setting the table for supper as she normally would, Naomi grabbed her mother's hand and led her to a chair. She wanted Ma to be sitting when she heard her news.

"Our prayers have been answered," she said. "I found a

way to pay for your surgery."

Though the growths had clouded Ma's eyes, there was no hiding the excitement that shone from them. "So soon? What happened?"

"I'm going to be an actress."

The excitement faded, replaced by confusion and disappointment. "I don't understand. You're a baker. How can you be an actress? You don't know anything about the stage."

Naomi realized the term she'd used so casually had created a problem when that hadn't been her intention. "Not on the stage. This is more of a private performance. Do you remember me telling you about Gideon Carlisle?"

Though she still seemed perplexed, Ma nodded. "The handsome young man who's having his portrait painted."

He was that and more. Much more. But Naomi had no intention of admitting how often her thoughts turned to Gideon. Instead, she patted her mother's hand as she said, "Gideon's faced with a dilemma." After she explained about Mrs. Carlisle's visit and edict, Naomi concluded, "So I agreed to pretend to be his fiancée while his mother is here."

Once again doubt colored Ma's expression. "Are you sure that's the right thing to do?"

"I am. I believe God gave me this opportunity to help you, but I need you to help, too. No one must know that it's a temporary engagement. We'll break it off quickly once Mrs. Carlisle leaves, but in the meantime it has to seem real.

That means you'll have to be an actress, too." It was true that Ma didn't leave the apartment very often, but once word of Naomi's supposed betrothal spread, it was likely that friends and acquaintances would visit.

"I'll try." Ma removed her spectacles and rubbed her eyes, then opened them wide as if trying to imagine what it would be like to see clearly. "You're right, Naomi. This opportunity seems like a miracle, but I wish it was a real engagement. More than anything, I want to see you settled with children of your own."

"I know, Ma. I know." But that wasn't going to happen. Not with Gideon.

"Good morning, Naomi." Though Gideon smiled, the smile didn't reach his eyes when he knocked on the door early the next morning. "I hope you haven't changed your mind."

It was an unusual greeting, but Naomi couldn't blame him. She'd wakened this morning wondering if their engagement had been nothing more than a dream. "I haven't changed my mind," she said, watching relief wash over him as she shook her head. "Come inside and meet my mother."

As she led him toward the table where Ma was still seated, Naomi could only imagine how the apartment appeared to a man who lived in a mansion. The main room, which served as dining room and parlor, was small, its furnishings shabby, but at least it was clean.

If the modest surroundings bothered him, Gideon gave

no sign. He smiled at Ma as he said, "I'm pleased to meet you, Mrs. Towson. Although our arrangement is unusual, I can assure you that I will do everything in my power to ensure that Naomi is not hurt by it."

Ma peered through her thick spectacles for what felt like an eternity before she nodded. "I trust you." The approval surprised Naomi. In the past it had taken her mother weeks to pass judgment on the men who wanted to court her daughter.

Rising from her chair, Ma looked at Gideon. "If you would like some time alone with Naomi, I'll be in the kitchen."

Gideon nodded. "There is one thing I want to do before we go to Madame Charlotte's. Perhaps you'd like to sit down."

Naomi flushed, realizing she'd been remiss in not offering him a seat. But when she settled on one of the chairs in the parlor area, Gideon remained standing. A second later he descended to one knee in front of her, looking so much like a genuine suitor that Naomi's breath caught.

"I would be honored if you would wear my ring," he said, pulling a square box from his pocket.

Though she hadn't thought of a ring, it made sense that she would need one as a tangible sign of the engagement. As Gideon lifted the lid, Naomi gasped. Not even in her dreams had she imagined such a magnificent piece of jewelry. "I've never seen anything so beautiful." Three perfectly matched stones, a ruby, a diamond, and a sapphire, were set in a simple gold band.

Gideon's relief was evident. "I hoped you'd like it. When I saw the red, white, and blue stones, I thought they'd be a nice reminder of this particular Fourth of July. It seems my timing was perfect, because Mr. Mullen had just finished the ring an hour or so before I came into the store."

Naomi stared at the ring as Gideon slid it onto her finger. "I don't know what to say. It's magnificent." Looking at it she could almost believe the engagement was real.

"Let's see if we can find some gowns to go with it."

They walked the three blocks to Élan, Madame Charlotte's dress shop, and Naomi felt as if she were living a dream. Here she was, simple Naomi Towson, strolling with her hand on cattle baron Gideon Carlisle's arm, his ring on her finger. Only in her dreams would that have happened.

Gideon rapped on the door to Élan, and one of the most striking women Naomi had ever met opened it. Though Madame Charlotte was about the same height as Naomi and had the same dark brown hair and eyes, the similarities ended there. Madame Charlotte's almost regal posture and the perfectly fitted gown made her look like a creature from a different world.

"Good morning, Mr. Carlisle." Though it bore no hint of a French accent, Madame Charlotte's voice was low and cultured. She smiled as she greeted Naomi, and while her eyes assessed her, Naomi saw no disdain for her clothing. "It will be a pleasure to dress you, Miss Towson. I have a few garments I think will suit you."

The dressmaker motioned Gideon to one of the chairs in the main room before leading Naomi into a dressing room where she'd hung three gowns. Though she called them simple day dresses, the intricate detailing of the seams and the addition of double box pleats around the hem made them anything but ordinary.

An hour later Naomi's head was spinning when she left the shop. As Madame Charlotte had predicted, two of the dresses needed only minor alterations, and one was a perfect fit. She'd insisted that Naomi wear that one. With its beautifully draped skirt edged in what the modiste told her was French lace, its small bustle, and the signature pleats, it was the most beautiful garment Naomi had ever owned. And the fancy gowns Madame Charlotte was planning to make for her were beyond anything she'd ever dreamed of.

"I feel like Cinderella getting ready for the ball," Naomi told Gideon as they strolled slowly down Ferguson Street.

"Don't worry," he said, his blue eyes sparkling with mirth. "My coach won't turn into a pumpkin."

But the engagement would end. That was how it had to be.

Gideon smiled as he handed Naomi into the carriage. The past two weeks had been more enjoyable than any he could recall. Though Naomi still worked in the bakery, Esther had agreed that she was only needed in the morning. That gave them afternoons to spend together.

Believing it was important that his colleagues saw him with Naomi before Mother arrived, he and Naomi had done the things any courting couple would. They'd taken walks through the parks and drives through town, and of course, they'd attended church services together.

Those hadn't been as bad as Gideon had feared. Instead of thunderbolts the sermons had touched on God's love. The way the parishioners had nodded had made Gideon wonder if he was the only one who didn't believe in God's love, but he wouldn't think about that today. Today would be the first true test of his and Naomi's acting abilities, for today was the day his mother arrived.

Though Naomi smiled when they arrived at the depot, she was unable to hide the faint trembling of her hand. Gideon gave her a reassuring smile, hoping to allay her concerns. "It'll be fine," he said.

She nodded and gestured toward the construction site. "I'm glad we're getting a new depot." It was an obvious attempt to change the subject from her nervousness.

Gideon agreed, both with her sentiment and the diversion. "It'll be more suited to a city of Cheyenne's stature." The old depot was a simple wooden structure, whereas the new one would be an impressive red sandstone edifice. "I'm surprised it took the Union Pacific so long to agree to build it, but there's no doubt that it will be beautiful when it's finished. Who knows? We may even have statehood by then."

A whistle announced the approaching train, and Naomi turned her attention to the passengers emerging from the iron horse. She wouldn't recognize Mother, but Gideon did. His smile broadened when he saw the familiar figure descend the steps. Mother looked no older than she had when he'd left home, but it appeared that she'd gained a few pounds and was now decidedly plump. Though her clothing was covered with dust from the long journey, she showed no sign of fatigue.

"Gideon!" Mother cried, opening her arms to greet him.

He suffered the hug and the cloud of perfume that surrounded him when she wrapped her arms around him, then turned toward Naomi.

"Mother, I'd like you to meet Miss Towson. Naomi has done me the honor of accepting my ring." He remembered Naomi's concerns about dishonesty and chose his words carefully.

For a second, Gideon thought his mother had misunderstood him, but as a grin spread across her face, he realized it had simply taken her a while to believe him.

"Is it true? You're really getting married?"

Rather than lie, he said, "That's the normal end of an engagement." Perhaps he was prevaricating, but Gideon didn't want to contribute to Naomi's discomfort. She gave him a quick smile as his mother approached her.

"Oh, my dear, let me look at you." Ignoring the other passengers who were still disembarking, Mother tipped her head to one side and gave Naomi a thorough appraisal. To his fiancée's credit, she did not flinch but simply smiled as if this were a common occurrence.

"You're a lucky man, Gideon, to have found yourself a girl as pretty as Naomi," Mother said when she'd completed her inspection. She turned back to Naomi. "You will let me call you that, won't you?"

"Certainly, Mrs. Carlisle."

Unsure what his mother would do or say next, Gideon gestured toward the baggage being unloaded from the back of the train. "Let's get your trunks into the carriage. I imagine you're tired from your journey and would like a chance to rest."

"Nonsense! I want to get to know my future daughter-in-law. Take us somewhere we can have a cup of coffee while we get acquainted."

Though the logical destination would have been Esther's bakery, Gideon didn't want to run the risk of other customers recognizing Naomi as the woman who used to serve them. Gideon wasn't ashamed of Naomi's work—how could anyone be ashamed of the delicious cakes she baked?—but he didn't want Mother to realize how sudden their engagement was. And so he took them to Mr. Ellis's Bakery and Confectionary.

Once inside, Gideon sat back, watching the two women. He no longer harbored any doubts about Naomi's ability to carry off the charade. She kept Mother entertained with anecdotes of how Cheyenne had grown and changed over the past few years, while Mother interjected her own stories of life in the East, leaving Gideon no need to do more than murmur an occasional assent. The day was turning out even better than he'd hoped.

"You've done well for yourself," his mother said at supper that evening. "Naomi is exactly the kind of woman I hoped you'd marry. I'm proud of you, Gideon."

He swallowed in a vain attempt to dislodge the lump that had taken residence in his throat. He'd wanted Mother's approval, but oh, how he wished it were not based on a sham.

Chapter 5

"Let me feel the fabric."

Naomi bit the inside of her cheek, trying not to cry. Here she was, dressing for dinner with Gideon and his mother at Cheyenne's most prestigious hotel, wearing the most beautiful gown she'd ever owned, and her mother could barely see it. Though neither of them discussed it, Naomi knew that Ma's eyesight was worsening. That was why she wanted to touch the fabric.

"Madame Charlotte told me it's dupioni silk that came all the way from China," Naomi said as she placed a fold of the sumptuous material in her mother's hands. By some small miracle, her voice bore no hint of the worry that weighed so heavily over her. If she'd had any doubt that her agreement with Gideon was the right thing to do, watching Ma's vision fail would have erased it. Naomi had to do whatever she could to restore her mother's sight.

Ma gave her a bittersweet smile as she stroked the

sapphire blue silk. "It must be wonderful to sew with fabric like this. Of course," she said with a chuckle, "my customers had nowhere to wear anything so fine. Now turn around so I can see that demi-train you've been telling me about."

When Ma had admired the drape of the gown, she sighed softly. "I wish I could see Madame Charlotte's store. All those beautiful fabrics and the dresses. . ."

That wish was easy to grant. "I'll take you there on Monday. I'm sure she'd be happy to show you around."

But Ma shook her head. "I can't do that. It wouldn't be right to take her time when I have no intention of buying anything from her." Ma's expression brightened at the sound of a knock on the door. "You just enjoy your evening. I expect you to tell me every detail."

As Naomi ushered Gideon into the apartment, he gave her an appreciative look and grinned. "I'll be the envy of every man in Cheyenne when I walk into the InterOcean with the most beautiful woman in all of Wyoming Territory on my arm."

Though his compliment made her flush with pleasure, Naomi couldn't accept it. "It's the gown. Madame Charlotte's creations flatter everyone."

"It's not the gown," Gideon said firmly. "Remember, I've seen you in your work clothes. You were just as fetching then."

The light flush turned into a full-fledged blush. "Are you trying to turn my head?"

He shook his head. "I'm simply telling the truth. Now, if you're ready. . ." He led her outside and helped her into the carriage where his mother was waiting.

"That's a lovely gown, Naomi. Did you order it from Paris?"

Naomi smiled at Mrs. Carlisle. Though they hadn't discussed what they'd be wearing tonight, Gideon's mother had donned a light blue silk gown that complimented Naomi's sapphire blue. "It's not from Paris. There's a wonderful dressmaker right here."

"I'm surprised."

Gideon chuckled as he flicked the reins. "Admit it, Mother. Almost everything about Cheyenne surprises you." He turned and gave Naomi a rueful smile. "Despite the letters I've written her, until she arrived here my mother believed everyone lived in tents and had a steady diet of pork and beans."

"I don't imagine that's on the menu at the InterOcean."

It wasn't. With its linen tablecloths, fine china, and silverware, the InterOcean's dining room lived up to its reputation as Cheyenne's most elegant eating establishment. The food was equally good, the menu featuring elk, venison, and trout in addition to a wide selection of beef dishes. Succulent vegetables and breads almost as delicious as Esther's made it an unforgettable meal, while the array of desserts surpassed anything Naomi had seen.

"You were right, Gideon," Mrs. Carlisle said as they savored the delicate crème brûlée they'd chosen to end the meal. "Cheyenne is not what I expected. It appears to be a fine place to raise a family."

She turned to Naomi. "Won't you tell me about your family? Do your parents live in Cheyenne? How many siblings do you have? Just call me a nosy old woman, but I want to know more about the woman who's going to marry my son."

Though the questions were far from intrusive, Naomi was uncomfortable with them, simply because she and Gideon hadn't discussed how to address the issue of her mother. Deciding that her only recourse was honesty, she said, "My father died five years ago, and I'm an only child."

Mrs. Carlisle took another sip of her tea. "That sounds as if your mother is still alive. Does she live in Cheyenne?" When Naomi nodded, Gideon's mother's face brightened. "Wonderful! I'd like to meet her."

They hadn't planned for this. Naomi shot Gideon a look, but his expression was inscrutable. She was on her own here. "My mother's eyesight is failing, and she rarely leaves our home."

"Surely she'll make an exception for me." Mrs. Carlisle turned to Gideon, the firm line of her lips confirming Gideon's statement that his mother was a determined woman. "Do your best, son, to persuade Mrs. Towson. I'd like the four of us to celebrate the Fourth of July together."

Gideon nodded. "I'll do what I can."

Though Naomi saw regret in her mother's eyes, her voice was firm as she said, "I'm sorry, Mr. Carlisle, but I don't believe that would be a good idea. I bump into things in unfamiliar places. I wouldn't want to embarrass you."

"I assure you, you wouldn't embarrass anyone. My mother is genuine in her wish to spend time with you."

Naomi bit back a smile at the evidence of Gideon's determination. If she were a betting woman, she would wager that Ma would capitulate.

Ma was not smiling as she plucked at her skirt. "It shames me to admit this, but I have nothing appropriate to wear to the Cheyenne Club."

Gideon had explained that the plans for the Fourth of July celebration included attending the parade and then dining at the private club where he and many of Cheyenne's wealthiest businessmen were members.

"Madame Charlotte can remedy that," he said smoothly.

Ma shook her head. "You know our situation." Though she didn't say "financial situation," the implication was clear.

Gideon would not be dissuaded. "I shall, of course, pay for your clothing as I did for Naomi's."

"That would not be proper." Ma had questioned the propriety of Gideon's buying Naomi's fancy clothing but had ultimately agreed that as long as no one other than Gideon and Madame Charlotte knew, it would not compromise Naomi's reputation.

"Surely a man is permitted to give his future mother-in-law a gift."

"But she's not your future mother-in-law." Though she'd been silent during the exchange, believing it was between Gideon and her mother, Naomi couldn't help interjecting her protest.

His eyes were serious as he said, "In the eyes of the world, she is." Turning to Ma, he continued his argument. "If you agree, you'd be making my mother very happy and giving Madame Charlotte additional income. Are you willing to deprive them?"

Though Ma hesitated, Naomi knew her mother was on the verge of agreeing. "All right, Mr. Carlisle."

"Gideon," he said firmly. "I insist you call me Gideon."

"All right, Gideon. I accept."

After she'd escorted Gideon to the door, Naomi turned to her mother. "Do you know what just happened?" Without giving Ma a chance to reply, she said, "Gideon made your wish come true. Now you have a reason to visit Élan."

"They're thick as thieves." Gideon gestured toward the two mothers who'd been talking practically nonstop since they emerged from church. This was the first time the women had met, and though Gideon had had fewer concerns than Naomi, he was still grateful that Mother had taken an immediate liking to Mrs. Carlisle. Despite the concerns she'd voiced about her vision, he had not noticed any hesitation when Naomi's mother walked into church, nor had she bumped into anything—or anyone—when they'd been at the parade.

Since the Fourth of July fell on a Sunday this year, the schedule had been altered slightly, with the parade delayed until noon to ensure that it did not conflict with worship. When the church service had ended, Gideon had taken the three women back to his house for what Preble termed a light repast, and from then on, his mother and Naomi's had acted more like long-lost friends than new acquaintances.

Gideon wasn't complaining. Far from it, for the older women's absorption in their own conversation meant that he could devote all of his attention to Naomi.

She was more beautiful than ever today, with that lovely dark hair arranged in some kind of intricate style. He wasn't sure how a woman would describe the dress she was wearing; all he knew was that it showcased her beauty. His heart had swelled with pride as he'd stood at her side during the parade, watching the marching bands, the school children, and the politicians make their way through the city streets. And now they were seated on the porch of the Cheyenne Club, waiting for dinner to be served.

"I haven't seen Ma this excited in years." Naomi kept her voice low, though Gideon doubted that either of their mothers would have overheard her.

"I could say the same thing about my mother." She'd

been content before, but today she was almost radiant with happiness. "Her visit is working out even better than I'd expected, and it's all because of you." Gideon leaned over and placed his hand on top of Naomi's. "Thank you, Naomi. This is turning into the best summer I can remember."

How he hated the thought that it would end.

Chapter 6

The aroma of bacon greeted Gideon as he descended the stairs, leading him into the dining room where he found his mother seated with a plate of bacon, eggs, and toast in front of her.

"Good morning, Mother," he said, wondering why she was downstairs half an hour earlier than normal. His mother was a creature of habit, and once she established a schedule, she rarely deviated from it.

She smiled and gestured toward his chair at the head of the table. "Indeed, it is a good morning." When he was seated and had poured himself a cup of coffee, she spoke again. "You were right when you told me I'd like Cheyenne. I do. So much, in fact, that I've decided to spend the whole summer here." She glanced at the door leading to the butler's pantry, as if expecting it to open. "Preble told me it's unusual to have snow before October, so I shall plan to leave on October 1."

Mother was staying? Gideon stared at her, realizing he hadn't been this shocked since the day he'd received her letter announcing her plans to come to Cheyenne to meet his bride-to-be. What was he going to do now? Mother was supposed to be here for two weeks, not more than three months.

Count your blessings. Gideon could practically hear his mother's admonition, and so he followed it. At least she hadn't decided to remain until the wedding. He'd be in a real pickle if she did that.

"Aren't you going to say something, son?" Mother wielded her knife and fork, cutting a slice of bacon into precise bite-sized pieces. As she slid one into her mouth, she lifted an eyebrow in a gesture Gideon knew meant that her patience was fading.

"I'm surprised." He wouldn't admit that he was shocked. "I thought you couldn't leave the Ladies Aid Society for more than a few weeks."

Mother's hand fluttered in a dismissive wave. "Nonsense. Gertrude Menger will do an excellent job leading them. She's been hoping for an opportunity to make some changes. This will be her chance." When she'd stirred a teaspoon of sugar into her tea, Mother nodded. "I'll send her a telegram today."

Gideon tried not to groan at the realization that this wasn't a passing fancy and that he would never dissuade her.

"What's the matter, Gideon? Don't you want me to stay?"

"Of course I do." It wasn't a lie. He enjoyed having

Mother here. It was simply that the pretend engagement complicated everything. "I'm concerned that I won't be able to entertain you properly. I have to go out to the range this week. My foreman does a good job, but I need to check on him and the hands occasionally."

Mother's smile brightened. "That won't be a problem. I can spend the time helping Naomi and her mother plan the wedding." As she spread jam on a piece of toast, Mother gave Gideon one of those "mother knows best" looks that he remembered from his youth. "I do wish you'd reconsider and have the wedding before I leave. Christmas Eve may seem romantic now, but there's nothing like being a summer bride."

Unbidden, Gideon pictured Naomi carrying a bouquet of wildflowers, smiling as she walked down the aisle toward him. He caught his breath, startled by the intense longing that rushed through him. Though the idea was more appealing than any he could recall, now was not the time to regard marriage the way a drowning man did a life preserver. When he married—if he married—it would not be merely to placate his mother. But though he tried his best, Gideon was unable to dismiss the image of a wedding—a real one.

"Gideon." Naomi was startled by the sight of him entering the bakery kitchen. Ever since she'd begun the pretend engagement, though she no longer served customers in the front room, she spent her mornings in the kitchen, helping Esther mix and knead the breads and pastries that were the bakery's mainstays. Never before had Gideon interrupted her.

Naomi washed her hands and turned toward him. "Is something wrong?" she asked, unable to read his expression.

When she'd seated herself, Gideon took a chair across from her at the table that served as both a work surface and a dining table for Esther and Jeremy. "I'm not sure. I hope not. How is your mother?"

Something was definitely wrong, because Gideon didn't normally dither. Naomi blinked at the non sequitur. "Ma's fine. This morning she told me again how much she enjoyed yesterday."

"So did mine." Gideon nodded, the corners of his mouth descending into a frown. "She enjoyed it so much that she's decided to extend her visit."

While Gideon was visibly uneasy with the idea, the jolt of happiness that spread its warmth throughout her shocked Naomi. Her heart sang at the realization that if Mrs. Carlisle remained in Cheyenne, Naomi would have a reason to continue spending time with Gideon. It was foolish—oh, so foolish—to care, and yet she did.

"How long does she plan to be here?" Naomi asked as calmly as she could.

"Until October first." Gideon's increasing discomfort told Naomi she was the only one who rejoiced in the prospect of more time together.

He leaned forward slightly, placing his forearms on the table. "I hope you'll agree to extend our arrangement. I know October is far later than we'd agreed, so I'll do more than pay for your mother's surgery. I'll set up a bank account for you and will deposit the same amount as the surgeon's fee into it now and then again in October when Mother leaves." His tone was as flat as if this were a business arrangement. But, of course, that was exactly what it was.

"No!" The word came out more forcefully than Naomi had intended. It hurt—oh, how it hurt—to be reminded that she was nothing more than an employee, even though that's what she was. Naomi bit the inside of her cheek, trying not to cry out in frustration. Their agreement had been clear. It was only she who'd thought she and Gideon were friends, or maybe even something more.

Gideon's eyes darkened with shock, and his face registered disappointment. "I know it's a lot to ask, but I need you, Naomi. Tell me what it'll take for you to agree."

"Nothing." He'd misunderstood her protest and had no way of knowing that she'd been insulted by his offer of money. "You don't owe me anything more. I agreed to be your pretend fiancée while your mother was here, and I will do that for however long she stays."

Unable to hide his relief, Gideon nodded then shook his head. "That doesn't seem fair. I feel as if I owe—"

"You don't owe me anything." Naomi cut him off. "You've already gone beyond our original arrangement by paying for my mother's clothes. She and I will probably need a few more dresses if we're to continue the charade until October. That will be enough."

But it wasn't. Naomi wanted a real engagement followed by a real wedding followed by life with Gideon. Unfortunately, what she wanted could never be.

Chapter 7

Gideon tried not to fidget. These minutes before the service began were always difficult for him. He knew he was supposed to focus on God, but instead his thoughts were whirling in a dozen different directions, reminding him of tumbleweeds in a storm. When they landed, it was often on the woman at his side.

Lowering his eyes, Gideon stared at the floor, trying to corral his thoughts. It had been more than a month since Mother had announced her extended stay. Though Gideon had been concerned by her insistence on helping with wedding plans, Naomi had managed to sidestep the issue, citing a reluctance to make any arrangements until after her mother's surgery. That was a valid-sounding reason, and Mother had accepted it.

She and Mrs. Towson had tea together every afternoon, talking endlessly. Gideon had no idea what they discussed and suspected he was better off not knowing. He wasn't complaining, though, for the time the two mothers spent sipping tea was time he had with Naomi.

The woman was amazing. His suppositions from before they'd begun their charade of an engagement had proven to be true. Each day found Gideon more fascinated by the woman who was pretending to be his fiancée. Naomi had a lively sense of humor and an open curiosity. She even seemed genuinely interested in his cattle. That made her the only woman he knew who could listen to stories about roundups and orphaned calves for more than a minute without her eyes glazing over.

When they were together, Gideon felt complete, as if Naomi filled the emptiness deep inside him. Perhaps that was the reason he thought of her so often and even dreamed of her. Perhaps that was the reason the time he'd spent on the range had seemed endless. Perhaps that was the reason he wanted to be with her, not just for the duration of his mother's visit but forever.

He closed his eyes and bit back a groan. It didn't matter how much he wanted Naomi as his wife. Gideon knew that would never happen, for there was an insurmountable obstacle between them: God.

An hour later, he tucked Naomi's hand into the crook of his elbow and escorted her down the church steps. "Why do you think God loves you?" he asked as they headed north on Ferguson, trailing the two mothers on their way back to Gideon's home. His question was more than an idle one. If he had any hope of breaking down the barrier to their life together, he needed to understand why Naomi was assured of God's love. Though Gideon felt peace steal over him during the services, he still had no evidence that God loved him.

Naomi looked up at him, her eyes so filled with joy that envy speared him. What must it be like to have such comfort? "I don't *think* God loves me," she said. "I *know* it."

"How? What happened to make you so sure?" This was a strange conversation to be having as they walked along one of Cheyenne's most elegant streets, nodding at passersby as they traveled the two blocks to Gideon's home, but an urgency he could not explain compelled him to keep probing.

Naomi paused and turned so she was facing him. This time her expression was solemn, as if she realized how important the discussion was. "I've seen the evidence. Whenever I most needed something, God provided."

Did she know how fortunate she was? Gideon hoped so, because his experiences had been far different. "Can you give me an example?"

"I'll give you two. You know my mother used to be a seamstress. Late last year her eyesight became so bad that she could no longer sew. At the same time, I lost my position as cook at the boardinghouse down the street. No matter how hard I tried, I couldn't find other work. Sooner than I thought possible, our savings were depleted. I didn't know what to do other than pray for help. That same day I saw a sign in the bakery window, saying that Esther was looking for an assistant. The money I made there kept Ma and me from being evicted."

It was no wonder Naomi's faith was so strong. Her prayers had been answered. Gideon's had not. "You said you had two examples."

She smiled, the sweetness of her smile setting his pulse to racing. "You were the second answer to prayer. I knew it would take a miracle to find the money to save Ma's sight, so I prayed for a miracle. The next day you proposed our engagement. That wasn't coincidence, Gideon. That was God's hand. He brought you into that bakery at exactly the right time to hear about my problem and then solve it."

Gideon had been told that God had a sense of humor. Perhaps this was an example of it, making a man like Gideon, a man who didn't believe in God's love, His instrument. "I can see why you believe that God was at work," he told Naomi. "The problem is, He's never once answered my prayers."

"Are you certain of that?"

Remembering his father's and brothers' graves, Gideon nodded. "I am."

"I can't believe I'm here." Though she'd admired the building that was one of Cheyenne's landmarks from the exterior, this was Naomi's first time inside the Opera House. The grand staircase, the chandelier with its fifty-two electric lights, and the skylights that loomed overhead were even more magnificent than she'd heard. "I feel like Cinderella again."

Gideon laid his hand over hers and squeezed it as he smiled. "You're more beautiful than Cinderella ever dreamed of being."

Though her pulse raced as much from the touch of his hand as his effusive words, Naomi pretended to be unaffected. "I keep telling you it's due to Madame Charlotte." Tonight's gown was a ruby-red creation with deceptively simple lines and intricate beading on the bodice. The combination was more than eye-catching. It was stunning.

Knowing this was probably the only chance she'd have to wear the gown and her sole opportunity to visit the Opera House, Naomi was determined to enjoy every minute of the evening. In little more than a month, Mrs. Carlisle would be on her way home, and the engagement would be over.

Naomi tried not to frown. She wished—oh, how she wished—that the engagement didn't have to end. Though she wasn't certain how or when it had happened, Naomi could not deny that her feelings for Gideon were deeper than she'd thought possible. Everything she did, every thought she had centered on him. When she was spreading filling on the cinnamon buns this morning, she thought of how Gideon would make a show of sniffing the air when he smelled their distinctive aroma. When she was dressing her hair tonight, she remembered how a lock had come loose one day and he'd touched it, telling her it was softer than the finest silk.

She'd even begun to dream of Gideon. The dreams were

always the same, with Naomi walking down the church aisle toward him, the smile on her face matching the joy she saw shining from his eyes. But the dreams invariably ended before she reached him.

Even though she woke with tears staining her cheeks, Naomi knew that was as it had to be. No matter how deeply she cared for him, she could not marry Gideon, just as she could not marry any man who dismissed God's love. She'd hoped and prayed that the time they spent in church and their discussions of God's grace would open Gideon's heart and that he would recognize all the gifts he'd been given, but so far it hadn't happened.

"Let's agree to disagree."

Naomi stared at Gideon in confusion. Had he read her thoughts? Of course he hadn't, she realized a second later. He was talking about her gown, not God's love.

"All right," she said with a forced smile. "I hope we don't disagree about the opera."

They did not. When it ended, they admitted that while they'd enjoyed the music, they both wished they'd been able to understand the lyrics.

"It's too nice a night to spend inside," Gideon said as they moved slowly down the staircase toward the exit. "Would you like to walk in the park?"

Naomi nodded. "City Park is one of my favorite places." Though it had been only four years since the city had planted trees, the cottonwoods had grown quickly. Combined with the curving paths and beds of flowers, they made it a lovely place to visit.

A few minutes later, Naomi and Gideon were strolling with her hand on his arm, admiring the flowers, talking about everything and nothing until they reached the center of the park. As if this was his destination, Gideon paused next to the fountain, then turned toward her. Though the night was moonless, the park's lights illuminated his face, revealing the uncertainty in his eyes. Whatever he was about to say worried him. Naomi wanted to reassure him, but she could not, for she was unable to read his thoughts.

"I told myself I would wait, but I can't wait another day." Reaching forward, Gideon took both of her hands in his. With one finger, he touched the ring on her left hand. "I know this was supposed to be a business arrangement, but it's become far more than that for me."

For her, too. Naomi's pulse began to leap at the thought that Gideon shared her feelings.

He took a shallow breath, exhaling as he said, "The way I feel about you has nothing to do with business. My heart races when I see you, and when we're apart, I can't think of anything but you. I love you, Naomi."

She had told him she felt like Cinderella, and she did—now more than ever. Naomi stared at the man she loved so dearly. Gideon was her very own Prince Charming, and here he was in one of the most romantic spots in Cheyenne, declaring his love.

"I don't want to live without you," he said, raising her hand to his lips and pressing a kiss on her gloved fingertips. "Will you make this a real engagement? Will you marry me?"

The happiness that swept through her shocked Naomi with its intensity. She'd never felt like this, never even dreamed that such happiness was possible. But, like Cinderella's night at the ball, it could not last. A second later, reality crashed through the fragile bubble of happiness.

"Oh, Gideon, I wish I could. I love you." She tugged one hand free and cupped his cheek, wanting him to know how deep that love was. "I want nothing more than to be your wife, but I can't." What separated them was far more important than a fairytale carriage being turned back into a pumpkin. What separated them was the matter of life and death, eternal life or never-ending death.

Tears welled in her eyes as she gazed at Gideon. "You know how important my faith is to me. No matter how much I love you—and I do love you—I cannot marry someone who does not share that faith. I'm sorry, Gideon. So sorry."

Chapter 8

Naomi's rejection hurt more than anything he could remember, more even than the time a bully had punched him in the stomach, knocking the breath from him. Gideon tried not to wince, but the pain was so deep it was physical. He shouldn't have asked her. Before tonight he'd had hope, but now that was gone, replaced by the bittersweet knowledge that she loved him as deeply as he did her but that they had no future.

That hurt. Oh, how it hurt! And yet Gideon was filled with admiration for her. Once again Naomi had proven to be a woman of unflinching integrity. No matter how it pained her, and he could see that it did, she would not compromise her principles.

"I'd give almost anything to change your mind," he told her, "but I won't lie to you."

The light from the street lamp cast shadows over her face, yet he could see the anguish in her eyes. "I know."

Gideon took Naomi's arm, suddenly eager to leave what he had thought would be a romantic spot. "I'm not sure what to tell my mother," he said as they walked toward the park's entrance.

"There's nothing to tell her. We'll continue as before until she leaves."

And they did. It must have been a convincing performance, because Mother had given no sign that she realized anything was different. It was only Gideon who knew that everything had changed. He'd had a glimpse of love and happily-ever-after, and it had been snatched from him. He wouldn't dwell on that. Not today. Today he had a call to make.

"This is most irregular." The white-haired doctor whom Doc Winston had introduced as Dr. Hibbard frowned. "I cannot discuss a patient's condition with someone outside the family."

Doc intervened, taking advantage of the fact that they were in his office and Naomi's mother was his patient. "Mr. Carlisle is soon to wed Mrs. Towson's daughter."

Though that wasn't true, Gideon had no intention of admitting that, especially not now. He needed to know what Naomi and her mother would be facing tomorrow. "Perhaps you could describe a hypothetical case, one with similar surgery, for a woman of Mrs. Towson's age. How long would such an operation take?"

Dr. Hibbard relaxed. "That's a perfectly valid question,

and one I'm happy to answer. If all goes well, such an operation should require no more than an hour. If there are complications, which sometimes occur, it could be up to two hours. Anything longer than that and the prognosis is dubious. Surgery of that length would indicate serious problems."

"And what might those problems be?" Gideon wanted to learn everything he could before he brought Naomi's mother here.

The older doctor listed a mind-numbing number of possible complications, all of which made Gideon's skin crawl. As if he'd seen Gideon's reaction, Doc Winston spoke. "We've both examined Mrs. Towson and have no reason to believe there will be complications."

"Have you explained everything to Naomi?"

Doc shook his head. "We don't want to worry her unnecessarily. I would suggest you follow our example."

Gideon did, even though it meant he'd passed a sleepless night. Today, despite Naomi's protests, he'd brought his carriage to their house and had escorted both her and her mother to the doctor's office. Now he was seated next to Naomi in the small waiting room while the two doctors attempted to save her mother's vision.

"You don't need to stay with me." Though she was unable to hide the fear in her eyes, Naomi's voice was calm. "I hate to think of your mother being alone."

"She's fine. As a matter of fact, she's having a fitting at

Madame Charlotte's today. I couldn't convince her that she has more than enough dresses at home, so she visited Élan yesterday and arranged an appointment."

Gideon didn't care how many gowns his mother bought, and he knew Naomi didn't, either. He was simply talking to avoid looking at his watch. The first hour had passed, and though he didn't want to know how long it had been since he'd last checked, he couldn't stop himself. Reaching into his watch pocket, he pulled out the fancy gold timepiece that had once been his father's and opened the case. As he had feared, it had been more than two hours since the surgery had begun. The doctors had found complications—serious complications.

Gideon looked at Naomi, his heart aching at the thought of what this could mean to her. Dr. Hibbard had been frank in saying that death was a very real possibility if the surgery extended too long. This had been much too long.

Gideon clenched his fists. He couldn't just sit here doing nothing. There had to be some way to help. But how? He knew nothing about medicine, and even if he did, Dr. Hibbard was the expert on this type of surgery. That was why Doc Winston had summoned him. If Dr. Hibbard couldn't help Mrs. Towson, no one could.

As his gaze rested on Naomi, Gideon knew that wasn't true. There was One with infinitely more power than Dr. Hibbard. According to Naomi, He answered her prayers. Though He'd ignored Gideon in the past, Gideon had to try. He had to do everything he could to help Naomi's mother.

"Is something wrong?" For the first time since they'd entered the waiting room, Naomi's voice registered concern.

"Why did you ask?" Gideon didn't want to answer directly for fear of frightening her.

"You look so solemn."

It was no wonder he looked solemn. He was more worried than he'd been in many years. "I want to pray," he admitted, "but I'm not certain how to begin."

Surprise flitted across Naomi's face, followed by unmistakable happiness. "You don't need fancy words. Just tell God what's in your heart."

Would He listen? Would He answer Gideon's prayers today? There was only one way to know. Gideon slid to his knees and bowed his head.

"I'm not sure You're listening," he said softly. "I wouldn't blame You if You weren't. What kind of child am I if I only talk to You when I need help?" There was no answer, but Gideon hadn't expected one. He continued. "I hope You're listening today, because Naomi's mother needs You. I ask that You guide the doctors. Show them what to do to restore her sight." He paused for a moment, searching for the words to express all that he felt. Swallowing deeply, he said, "I know You have the power to do this."

As he murmured an amen, Gideon felt peace settle over

him like a warm blanket on a cold night. He didn't know how long he knelt there, feeling lighter and freer than ever before, but gradually the feeling changed as images floated through his brain.

He remembered the morning he'd broken his arm and heard the doctor say it might not heal properly, but it had. Then there was the afternoon he'd found Mother weeping after Father and his brothers died. Gideon hadn't known how to comfort her, but the next day a stray dog appeared on their doorstep. That dog became Mother's companion and brought her the comfort her son hadn't been able to express. And then there'd been the day Gideon had worried about how to satisfy Mother's demand that he find a bride and how Naomi's inability to pay for her mother's surgery had occurred at exactly the same time.

A smile crossed Gideon's face as he realized how wrong he'd been. God had answered his prayers all along. He simply hadn't recognized it. Gideon might never understand why God had let Father and his brothers die, but he knew as surely as the September sun was shining outside that there had been a reason. A good reason. And he knew that God had heard his prayer for Naomi's mother and that He would answer it. . .in His way.

Though she didn't want to intrude on what was obviously a private moment, Naomi couldn't help watching Gideon. He knelt there, a broken and battered man, but when he raised his head, the tension that had marked his face was gone, replaced by what she could describe only as peace. Gideon's prayers had been answered, and so had hers: the man she loved had opened his heart and let God in. Closing her eyes, Naomi uttered a silent prayer of thanksgiving.

It was perhaps five minutes later that Gideon rose and reached for Naomi's hands, drawing her to her feet. "You were right," he said, his voice so filled with joy that she wanted to weep from sheer relief and happiness. "God does answer prayer. Not only yours, but mine, too. I was just too blind to see that."

Tears of joy welled in her eyes, and Naomi felt her throat thicken. Somehow she managed to speak. "Oh, Gideon. I'm so happy."

"And you haven't even heard my news."

They both turned at the sound of Doc Winston's voice. His smile and the relaxed lines of his face left no doubt of the outcome.

"The surgery was successful." Naomi made it a statement rather than a question.

"Yes. I won't deny that it was challenging. The disease had progressed further than either of us had realized, but Dr. Hibbard is confident that your mother will make a complete recovery. It will take several weeks before she can resume all her normal activities, but she should notice improvement every day."

"Thank you, Doc." Gideon extended his hand to the doctor.

As the doctor shook Gideon's hand, he nodded. "Mrs. Towson will be asleep for some time. There's no need for you and Naomi to remain here. Why don't you come back in three or four hours? I imagine you have other things to do."

"We do."

Gideon stared at Naomi, his surprise evident. "We do?"

"I thought we'd take a walk in the park," she said as they left the doctor's office. The moment she'd seen Gideon's face when his prayer ended, Naomi had known what she needed to say. Now she was being given the opportunity to do it in the perfect setting.

Though Gideon appeared bemused by the request, he handed her into the carriage and drove to City Park's perimeter, seemingly unfazed when she promised to explain only when they reached their destination.

Once they entered the park, Gideon let Naomi lead the way. Though he said nothing, she wondered if he realized they were retracing the steps they'd taken the night he'd asked her to marry him and if he had an inkling of what she planned to say.

It had been weeks since that night, weeks of pretending that nothing was wrong when her heart had been breaking. Had Gideon felt the same way, or had he changed his mind? She'd soon know.

When they reached the center of the park, Naomi stopped and looked up at Gideon. Though her heart was racing, to her amazement, her voice did not quaver when she spoke. Keeping her gaze fixed on him, she said, "The last time we were here, you asked me a question and I gave you an answer neither one of us liked. If you ask me again, my answer will be different."

A light breeze fluttered the cottonwood leaves while a ground squirrel scampered at their feet. Though it was an ordinary day in the park for others, Naomi could scarcely breathe while she waited for Gideon's response. Her future happiness hung in the balance.

The wait wasn't long—perhaps no more than a second or two—but Naomi felt as if an eternity passed before he spoke. "I'm not the same person I was then," Gideon said solemnly. "Many things have changed, but one thing has not, and that's my love for you. I love you with all my heart."

Gideon paused and laid one hand on Naomi's cheek, mirroring the gesture she'd used the last time they'd stood here. This was what she'd hoped for. Gideon loved her as much as she loved him.

The sweetest of smiles curved his lips as he said, "I love you, Naomi, and I always will. Will you make me the happiest man alive? Will you marry me?"

Yes! Yes! Yes! Though the words wanted to tumble out, Naomi found herself asking, "When?"

She couldn't blame Gideon when he blinked in surprise.

That was not the answer he'd been expecting. "What do you mean?"

"When would you like us to be married?" As they'd entered the park and the summer sun had warmed her back, Naomi had realized that she did not want a long engagement. Though they'd been pretending to court, she and Gideon had spent more than three months doing the things an affianced couple would. They knew each other, and now that the final obstacle had been removed, there was no reason to delay the wedding.

A mischievous grin crossed Gideon's face. "How about today?"

As appealing as the idea was, Naomi did not want to marry without her mother at her side. It would be a few days before Ma would be ready for that.

"I was thinking about next week," she said. "While you were out on the range, your mother did her best to convince me that I should be a summer bride. We still have seven more days of summer, so if we married next week, both of our mothers could be with us, and I could be a summertime bride."

Gideon's eyes shone with happiness and so much love that Naomi caught her breath. "Sweetheart, I'll marry you whenever and wherever you want." As a mischievous smile crossed his face, he wrinkled his nose. "There is one problem, though. You still haven't answered my question. Will you marry me?"

Naomi's giggle turned into a laugh. "Of course I will. I love you, Gideon—now and forever." And then, though it might scandalize anyone passing by, she raised her face for his kiss. This was Gideon, the man she loved, the man God had brought into her life to make her dreams come true. Together they would share a life of love and happiness, a life that would begin the day she became a bride of summer.

Amanda Cabot is the bestselling author of more than thirty novels and half a dozen novellas, including Jeremy and Esther's story, *The Christmas Star Bride*, and *Waiting for Spring*, which tells Madame Charlotte's story. Although she grew up in the East, a few years ago Amanda and her high school sweetheart husband fulfilled a life-long dream and are now living in Cheyenne. In addition to writing, Amanda enjoys traveling and sharing parts of her adopted home with readers in her Wednesday in Wyoming blog. One of Amanda's greatest pleasures is hearing from readers, and so she invites you to find her online at www.amandacabot.com.

THE COUNTY
FAIR BRIDE

by Vickie McDonough

Chapter 1

Bakerstown, Missouri
May 20, 1892

T he slowing train screeched like Aunt Louise did whenever she encountered a mouse. Prudence Willard smiled at the image her thought provoked, but as she stared at the Bakerstown Depot, growing bigger with each yard she traveled, all humor fled. Her stomach churned faster while the train decreased its speed. Would her mother be waiting? In light of the illness Prudy's father was experiencing, more than likely her mother would not. Dare she hope some of her friends would be there to greet her? Did they even know she was returning?

Prudy sat back in the seat. She dreaded facing the townsfolk after her shameless pursuit of Clay Parsons, the town's only pastor. And to think she'd attempted to get Clay's fiancée—Karen Briggs, who was now his wife—to leave town. And she almost did. She'd treated the kind woman horribly, and it would serve her right if not a soul showed up to welcome her home.

The train shuddered to a stop, like a beast of burden exhausted from a long journey. Several people picked up their satchels and headed for the door. A part of Prudy wished she could keep on riding down the track, but she needed to see her father. They'd never been close, but he was gravely ill, and she hoped she might be able to cheer him during his remaining days on earth. Heaving a sigh, she rose, picked up her travel bag, and headed for the door.

As she debarked the train and searched the platform, her hopes of a cheerful welcome plummeted. She didn't see a soul she knew. With a sigh, she walked down the platform and handed the porter the baggage-claim ticket for her trunk. A few minutes later, after making arrangements for her belongings to be delivered to her parents' home, she picked up her satchel and headed for the stairs. Just as she reached the top, a man dressed in a gray sack coat and trousers rushed up the stairs, his gaze directed toward the train. Since he was obviously in a hurry and hadn't spotted her, she stepped back, lest he run her down.

The man buzzed past her as he reached the platform. Suddenly he halted and spun around. A pair of deep blue eyes, set in a handsome face, turned her way and widened. He yanked off his straw hat, releasing his thick, dark hair, which tumbled onto his forehead. He moved forward, forking his hair across his head. "Miss Willard?"

More than a little intrigued, Prudy nodded. "Yes. And who might you be?"

His cheeks flushed a bright red as he replaced his hat. "I'm Adam Merrick. Your mother asked me to see you home since she didn't want to leave Mr. Willard. . .uh . . .your. . .uh. . .father alone."

Prudy bit back a smile at the flustered man, who looked to be only a few years older than herself. She couldn't resist teasing the befuddled man. "I do know who Mr. Willard is."

"Uh. . .of course." He offered his elbow. "Shall we?"

"Yes, thank you. I'm quite anxious to see how my father is faring." She looped her arm around his and glanced up. "Do you know how he is doing?"

The man's lips firmed as he pressed them together. "You should probably consult your mother concerning that."

She nodded. Turning to the stairs, she released his arm and shifted her satchel to her other hand so that she could hold onto the railing as she descended. The last thing she wanted to do was fall flat on her face in front of her shy but charming escort.

"Do allow me to carry that." He suddenly snatched the bag from her. "I'm sorry for not offering in the first place."

Thrown off balance, Prudy hovered on the top step, toes hanging over, and flapping her arms. Like a duck stuck in the mud, her efforts availed her little. Mr. Merrick dropped her satchel onto the edge of her skirt and yanked her toward him, away from the drop-off. Her foot hit the bag, and she fell hard against his chest, taking them both to the ground. A woman behind them gasped. Prudy pushed against his solid chest, wrestling her tangled skirts, and struggled to sit.

Less encumbered, Mr. Merrick hopped up. "I'm terribly sorry, Miss Willard. I really don't know how that happened."

Prudy refrained from fussing at him. Even flustered, the man certainly was comely, but she wasn't attracted to his bumbling manner in the least. "I don't suppose you could help me up."

"Oh! Um. . .certainly." He shoved his hand in front of her face, and she took it. He proved quite capable, hoisting her back onto her feet. She avoided looking at him and straightened her skirts. Peeking around the depot, cheeks blazing, she was relieved to note they were the only ones left. Thank goodness only a few people witnessed her humiliating stumble.

She was of a mind to give him a good tongue-lashing, but she was trying to change her ways. Better to pretend the embarrassing deed never happened. Needing distance, Prudy bypassed her satchel, grabbed hold of the railing, and safely descended the stairs. At least she hadn't fallen down them. The last thing her mother needed was for her to show up in need of care. The year and a half with Aunt Louise had helped her grow up and see how selfish she once was. She shivered at the thought of how rudely she'd treated others.

Though glad to be home, she couldn't deny she had many reservations. Would the townsfolk give her a chance to prove she was different? Or would they assume her to be the same sometimes cruel woman she had once been?

Mr. Merrick hurried to catch up with her quick steps.

"I assume by the quick pace you're keeping you weren't injured." He shifted her bag to his other hand and reached for her elbow, tugging her to a stop when she'd have trotted across the street in front of a nearby wagon. "What's the rush, Miss Willard?"

To get away from you before some other reprehensible event occurs. "I'm anxious to see my parents, of course."

"Well, it won't do for you to get run down by a buckboard before you see them."

She jerked free of his hold and lifted her chin. "I didn't plan on getting run over."

Instead of being taken aback, he had the audacity to grin. He pushed his hat back on his head. "And I bet you didn't plan to fall at my feet the first time we met."

Prudy sucked in a breath. The bumbling fool had been replaced by a rogue—and she didn't know which one she liked the least. She attempted to snatch her bag from his hold, but he refused to let go. She glared at him, but inside she secretly admired the vivid blue of his eyes, only a few shades darker than her own. Who was Adam Merrick? And how did he know her parents?

She blinked. She was staring too long.

Spinning, she picked up her skirts and made a beeline for her house. The sooner she was away from this intriguing, insufferable man, the better.

Adam watched the princess sashay toward her castle for a moment then rushed once again to catch up with the feisty woman. Mr. Willard had warned him his daughter could be as blunt as the hot end of a branding iron—her fiery tongue stung as much. He smiled at the man's comment. Prudy Willard was feisty, that was for sure, but she hadn't been rude or cruel—not even when he'd caused her to fall down and create a spectacle. He suspected her father was exaggerating a tad bit.

He blew out a loud sigh. Being late to greet her certainly wasn't the way to impress the lady, not that he wanted to. Still, since he'd taken over her father's job as mayor of the town, he was sure to see her on a regular basis and would like to be on friendly terms. But as she hurried to get away from him, he doubted she would be eager to see him again.

Her father should have warned him of her beauty. He'd been so taken off guard when he first saw her that he'd been tongue-tied—and he had never been accused of that before. She must think him a bumbling fool.

Ah well. What did it matter? He had a job to focus on—guiding this town and preparing it to ease into the twentieth century. He had no business worrying what a blond-haired, blue-eyed beauty thought of him.

His head was full of ideas for improving the town's business structure and bringing more money to Bakerstown, and he'd love to see electricity brought to the town by the turn of the century. He even had an idea for bricking the streets so that the townsfolk no longer had to walk through a quagmire after a heavy rainfall. Surely the women would appreciate such a gesture. But Bakerstown was a small town, and as such, his annual budget was minuscule.

Adam dodged a pile of fresh manure and caught up with Miss Willard. A pair of lovely blue eyes flicked his direction then quickly away. He wasn't sure what he'd expected in Prudence Willard, but her name had him imagining a book lover in a drab dress with glasses and a bun so tight it pulled her eyes into slits. Instead, her pretty hair, the color of corn silk, poofed around her face in a very feminine manner. Behind her, thick locks hung in dangling ringlets. His foot hit a rock. Adam took several quick steps and righted himself as heat marched up his neck. Miss Willard stopped in front of the gate to her parents' yard and eyed him like he was three-day-old trout. He picked up her satchel and dusted it off, then cleared his throat and motioned to the gate. "Allow me."

She stepped back with a loud sigh. Adam opened the gate and held it for her to pass through, never having felt so inept. No one would know he'd graduated from Briar Glen College at the top of his class with a business degree. It's what had allowed him to get the job as the mayor's assistant in the first place.

As he helped Miss Willard up the porch steps, he shook his head. What had started out as a beautiful day had ended up as one of the worst of his life.

Chapter 2

Prudy rushed into her mother's arms, glad to finally be home. She'd wanted to return around Easter, but the town had been dealing with an influenza outbreak, and her mother wouldn't hear of her coming back until it was over. Then her father came down with that awful illness, and Mother had postponed her return once again.

"How is Papa? Any better?"

Her mother stepped back, shaking her head. "I'm afraid not." She looked past her daughter, and her gaze lit up. She slipped around Prudy. "Mr. Merrick, I can't thank you enough for seeing Prudence home."

"It was my pleasure, Mrs. Willard." His gaze shot to Prudy and back to her mother. "Where would you like me to put your daughter's satchel?"

"Just set it on the hall tree bench. I'll have Clarence take it upstairs."

Mr. Merrick did as ordered then stood in the foyer

holding his hat. "Forgive me, but did I hear you say Emmett—uh. . .Mr. Willard is no better?"

Helen Willard nodded. "He had a rough night—trouble sleeping."

"Then I won't ask to see him." He looked at Prudy. "It was a pleasure to meet you, Miss Willard. I look forward to seeing you again." He donned his hat and gave a slight bow toward her mother. "Good day, Mrs. Willard."

"Thank you again for bringing Prudence home, and if Emmett is doing well on Friday, I'll expect you and your sister for dinner."

Mr. Merrick smiled. "Thank you, ma'am, but I don't want to be a bother."

Prudy watched in surprise as her mother touched Mr. Merrick's arm. "No bother. You know Emmett enjoys your visits and hearing about your week."

"Jenny always enjoys the time, too." He shot a quick glance toward Prudy, touched the end of his hat, and spun toward the stairs. Helen closed the door then turned and stared at Prudy. "You're a bit taller, I believe—and you've lost some weight. Did Louise not feed you properly?"

"Of course she fed me well." Prudy hated the rivalry between her mother and Aunt Louise. Though sisters, the two were completely different. Why couldn't her mother be as sweet and gracious as Louise? "What's this about Mr. Merrick and his sister coming for dinner?"

"When your father had the stroke after his severe sickness,

Mr. Merrick was elected interim mayor, and he's tried hard to keep Emmett informed of all he's doing, even though it's not required of him."

"Does he need Papa's guidance in order to do the job properly? I have to say he seemed quite a bumbling fool today."

Her mother cocked her head, looking perplexed, and then she smiled. "Adam must have been disarmed by your beauty. I've always found him to be quite capable."

Prudy decided her mother must be enamored with Mr. Merrick's comeliness. It wasn't like her shrewd mother to admire the very person who'd taken over her husband's job. That must be it.

She glanced up the stairs. "Is Papa awake? I'm anxious to see him."

Her mother pursed her lips and gave a brief shake of her head. "No, I'm afraid he was sleeping a few moments ago, just before I came downstairs." Helen looped her arm through Prudy's. "I have tea ready in the parlor. Come."

She hadn't been home two minutes, and her mother was already telling her what to do. She forced herself to relax, knowing her mother had missed her. And tea would taste good, especially if it were cold. Though it was only late May, the temperature was already quite warm. "Tea sounds wonderful. Thank you, Mother."

Helen beamed as she guided Prudy into the parlor. "So, tell me, how is that sister of mine?"

"Aunt Louise is well. She wanted to accompany me, but with Papa still ill, she thought it best to wait. She may come this fall and stay with Aunt Loraine."

"That was thoughtful of her to wait."

Thoughtful was a good word to describe her kindhearted aunt. Her mother was a busybody, always trying to tell people what to do or how to act, but Aunt Louise was quiet and preferred baking a pie to intruding in someone else's business. Prudy sighed.

While her mother filled her in on the town's activities, Prudy's thoughts turned to Adam Merrick. As interim mayor, he was to oversee the town until her father could return to work. He hardly seemed capable of such a task. Maybe she should talk with her father and then visit Mr. Merrick at the office to make sure he wasn't overstepping his authority.

"Prudence, you're not listening."

She blinked, sorry she had gotten caught lost in her thoughts. "I'm sorry, you said someone was with child?"

Her mother nodded, smiling wide. "Pastor Clay's wife is in the family way."

"That's. . .uh. . .nice." Prudy sat back in her chair. The man she'd once hoped to marry would be a father soon. And the woman who'd ruined her dreams would hold his child in her arms. She sighed. Aunt Louise told her she needed to put aside her disappointment of not marrying Clay Parsons and look to the future. Prudy had been able to do that at her aunt's home, but now that she was back and would surely face the two who had broken her heart, it was much harder. "So, is there still only one church in town?"

"Yes, I'm afraid so." Her mother reached across the table and laid her hand on Prudy's arm in an uncharacteristic show of emotion. "I realize it may be hard for you to face Pastor Parsons and Karen, but it's best to just do it and get it over with. I've found they are both kind, forgiving people."

"Perhaps I'll sit with Papa while you attend church."

"No, that won't work. Dr. Blaylock comes to play chess with Emmett every Sunday morning—at least they play when Emmett is able."

There would be no escaping her fate. Suddenly, Prudy felt as wrung out as a mop. "So, tell me about Papa. Is he getting any better?"

Her mother's lips tightened into a straight line. "I wish I could say yes, but the truth is, he's worse, if anything. He hasn't been able to regain his strength. His severe case of influenza would have been fatal to a weaker man, and then he had the stroke before he had a chance to fully recover." Helen batted her lashes and stared out the parlor window. "I don't know how I'll go on if—"

Prudy rose and hurried around the table, bending down to hug her mother. "Don't think of that now. We'll pray and do what we can each day to help Papa and try not to worry about the future."

A few minutes later, Prudy stepped into her frilly, pink bedroom. It looked like something that belonged to a young girl. She took a slow spin, studying the pink-and-white-striped draperies with rows of ruffles, the matching quilt, and the striped sofa and pink side chair. She felt as if she had walked into a peppermint stick factory. Before she left town, she had loved the bright room, but now it left her nauseated. Had she really changed so much?

Perhaps her mother would allow her to paint and make some other changes. It would give her something to do—besides overseeing Mr. Merrick.

The next morning, Prudy strode into the mayor's office. The door made a familiar click as she closed it. Most of her teen years, her father had been mayor, and she'd visited him here many times after school before heading home. Even though she knew Adam Merrick was more than likely using her father's desk as his own, seeing him sitting there still rattled her.

He glanced up from perusing a stack of papers and popped to his feet so fast, the papers went flying. Mr. Merrick made a comical sight as he grabbed for several pages in midair and slapped them on the desk, ignoring those that fluttered to the floor. He snatched up his frock coat, which had been lying across one end of his desk, and shoved his arms into it. "Miss Willard, how nice to see you again. Might I inquire after your father?"

Prudy looked around the office, attempting to regain her composure. She hadn't counted on noticing how nicely Adam Merrick filled out the crisp white shirt he wore. Shifting her gaze away from him, she noticed a college diploma hung where her father had nailed up an award he'd received from the town. There were other subtle changes. Was Mr. Merrick taking over when his job was temporary? Turning her thoughts to her father instantly sobered her. "I fear he's worse off than I expected, but I'm hoping he will rally now that I'm home and can take some pressure off his shoulders."

He picked up a paper, set it on the desk, and moved toward her, compassion filling his eyes. "I'm sorry you couldn't have received better news, Miss Willard." He gestured at a chair sitting in front of his desk. "Would you care to sit?"

"Yes. Thank you." He held on to the back of her chair as she lowered herself onto it, then he returned to his seat on the far side of the large desk. "To what do I owe the pleasure of your visit?"

Prudy stared at her lap, irritated that she'd noticed the intriguing dimple that winked at her when Mr. Merrick smiled. His kindness would only make her task more difficult. She drew in a breath then lifted her head. "I'll be honest. I was stunned to find my father so wasted away. He is a shell of the man he was when I left town, a year and a half ago."

He pursed his lips. "I truly admire your father and enjoyed

the year we worked together. He's quite intelligent and has a heart for this town. It's been hard to watch such a vibrant man go downhill." He tugged at his collar, his ears turning red. "Uh. . .pardon me, Miss Willard. I probably shouldn't have said that."

Prudy stared at him, watching him squirm. "Well, it is true. That's why I've come today. Instead of visiting with my father in the future, you may talk to me, and I'll relay the information to him that I feel is warranted."

He blinked, looking confused. "I was under the impression your father enjoyed my visits."

"I'm sure he does, but I believe they are overtaxing him. I think he will improve quicker if I act as mediator."

He cleared his throat. "Things have been going fine without your interference."

Prudy stiffened, taken off guard by his harsh tone. "I disagree."

He rose and tugged on the bottom of his coat. "Regardless, you are not the mayor."

She hiked her chin. "Need I remind you that you are only the *interim* mayor?"

He rounded his desk. "Appointed by the town council. And might I add that your father wholeheartedly endorsed my taking over for him."

Prudy rose, struggling for a comeback. "Well, he was ill at the time."

Mr. Merrick's nostrils flared. "Thank you for taking the

time to visit, but as you can see, I have work to do."

She glanced at several papers still on the floor and lifted a brow. "Indeed."

He glared at her for a long moment then blew out a loud breath. "I'm not trying to replace your father, Miss Willard, so you can relax your ruffled feathers. I do, however, plan to do the best job that I can until he returns."

She hadn't expected his acquiescence, and it momentarily disarmed her. Maybe he didn't realize he wanted to take over, but he was having the same effect. She was certain he was part of the reason her father was still ill. The man was doing too good of a job, and her father felt he no longer had anything to live for. And she couldn't tolerate that. "I plan to return tomorrow to help you."

His mouth dropped open. "I don't need your assistance. My sister does the filing and serves as my typist."

"Nonetheless, I will see you tomorrow." Prudy rushed toward the door, her heart pounding. She hadn't planned on becoming Adam Merrick's partner when she left home. What had gotten into her?

Adam stared at the closed door, unable to move. Talk about a whirlwind. Emmett had warned him that his daughter could be headstrong, but never once had he considered she'd resent him for stepping up as mayor when no one else wanted the position. The salary was so minimal he had to supplement his income by keeping books for several businesses and auditing the bank quarterly. And the town's annual budget was so puny, he barely had the funds to replace the nails that came loose from the boardwalk.

He sighed and walked to the window. This job certainly didn't pay enough if he had to work with Prudence Willard on a daily basis, no matter if the fire in her eyes stirred him in a way he didn't like.

But he promised Emmett he'd keep the town running smoothly until the man recovered. Although, from the look of things, that might not happen for a long while. They'd discussed ways to improve the town's coffers, but the only viable solution Adam could come up with was to hold a county fair. So far, no town in the county had one, and if Bakerstown could be the first, the town stood to earn a lot of badly needed income.

Adam rubbed the back of his neck and looked out the window, gazing up at the sky. "I could use some help here, Lord. What am I supposed to do with Emmett's daughter?"

The door rattled, and Adam stiffened, fully expecting Prudence Willard to return and give him another tongue-lashing.

"Who was that woman I saw leaving?"

Jenny—not Prudence. Adam blew out a breath and relaxed. He smiled at his sister. "That was Emmett's daughter, Prudence."

Jenny's brown eyes widened as she lifted her hand to

cover her lips. "So she has returned. I hate to admit it, but I've heard some dreadful things about her. What did she want?"

He shrugged. "I think she believes I'm trying to take over her father's job, and she resents that." He didn't want to confess she also blamed him for her father not recovering. Could there be a thread of truth in that idea? If Emmett thought he didn't have a job to return to, it might affect his recovery. The first chance he got, he needed to reassure the man. Although Adam enjoyed serving as mayor, there were other things he could do to earn an income.

Jenny removed her hat and gloves. "She's much prettier than I expected."

Adam nodded. "You should see how her eyes blaze when she's angry."

His sister cocked her head, eyebrows lifted.

He knew that look and waved his hands in the air. "Don't go getting any ideas about matchmaking. She is a pretty woman, and I'd not be a man if I didn't notice. That doesn't mean I'm attracted to her."

"Hmm. . ." A smile graced his sister's lips as she set her gloves on the small table that served as her desk.

"Don't *hmm* me, Jenny. And might I remind you that your job is filing, not finding me a wife."

She didn't respond but rather thumbed through the papers he'd left for her, that ornery smile still on her lips.

He grabbed the last of the papers that had flown from his

hands when Prudy first stormed in. He didn't have enough tasks to keep Jenny busy. How was he going to manage to find work for Prudy, too?

And how was he going to get anything done with her lavender scent filling his office?

He wouldn't.

He'd just have to find a way to get rid of her.

Fast.

Chapter 3

Prudence Willard arrived promptly at ten o'clock, and an hour later, Adam was ready to resign as mayor. He heaved a sigh. "Miss Willard, surely you're wise enough to realize that Bakerstown is too small to support an opera house."

"I'm well aware of the town's size, Mr. Merrick. I have lived here most of my life, unlike you." She smirked as if thinking she'd landed a killing blow with her last comment. "An opera house would bring in money our town desperately needs."

He took a step toward her. "Only if people are willing to travel a great distance to get here. And once they are here, where would they stay? We don't even have a hotel." He blew out a sigh. "Where are we supposed to get the money to build such a facility?"

Prudy blinked several times, and he could almost see the wheels spinning in her mind. She snapped her fingers. "If we built a hotel with a restaurant, we could earn even more income."

Adam pinched the bridge of his nose and glanced at his wide-eyed sister. Jenny had hardly uttered a word since Emmett's daughter arrived. "Jenny, please tell Miss Willard how much money is in the town treasury."

"After we pay Mr. Michaels for repairing the boardwalk where the wood rotted, we'll have one hundred and three dollars and sixty-two cents."

Prudy's eyes widened. "How can there be such a trivial amount? Surely there's more." She stepped close to Adam, glaring at him. "What have you spent it all on?"

He resisted rubbing his forehead where an ache was building. "Did your father share with you how much was in the bank account when he was mayor?"

"Um. . .well. . .no. But there certainly had to be much more than that."

"There wasn't, I'm sorry to say. That's why I'm trying so hard to come up with an idea to bring in additional funds."

"I don't understand. Surely my father made a decent salary. Otherwise, how could my parents have afforded such a nice home?"

Did she not know about her father's inheritance from his uncle? Emmett had once confided that was how he kept his two women happy and living far above their current means. He never could have afforded such a nice home on his mayoral salary. But that wasn't his news to share. "You'll have to ask your father about that, I'm afraid."

"Believe me. I will." She lifted her chin. "So, back to

raising money. What wonderful ideas have you come up with?"

Adam stuck his finger in his collar and tugged. Why did it feel as if it were choking the life from him? "I think we need to concentrate on getting new businesses to come to town, which will generate more money in taxes. Then we should focus on improving the streets and maybe even bring electricity to Bakerstown."

Prudy crossed her arms. "Just how do you plan to entice those businesses to come to town? I've been gone a year and a half, and as far as I can tell, there are no new ones."

Jenny rose and cautiously approached them. "You have to understand, Miss Willard, Adam has only been the interim mayor for half that time, and a good chunk of it was spent learning his duties and getting to know most of the townsfolk so that he could understand how to best serve them. And he does have his other jobs to attend to."

He cut a sharp glare at his sister as Prudy's head jerked toward him. He hadn't wanted her to know about his other places of employment.

"You work somewhere else, besides fulfilling your mayoral duties? How can you expect to prosper the town when you don't devote your full attention to it?"

"Oh dear. I'm sorry, Adam." Jenny turned and fled to her small desk. "I. . .uh. . .need to. . .uh. . .run an errand." She snatched up her reticule and rushed out the door.

He felt like a lily-livered cad for making her feel bad.

He owed her an apology. But first he had to deal with Miss Willard, who was quickly becoming as bothersome as a splinter underneath a fingernail. He straightened, taking advantage of his height to force her to look up. "The truth is, this job doesn't pay enough to support my sister and me, so I have no choice but to work other places."

"What kind of places?"

He lifted a brow. "That, Miss Willard, is none of your concern. I can assure you, though, that my other duties do not affect my performance as mayor."

"Interim mayor."

He pursed his lips to keep from saying something he'd regret. He'd devoted many hours to this town for a pittance of a salary, and he didn't appreciate her attitude. He'd never met a woman so obstinate—so interesting. Adam swallowed, appalled by that last thought. Yes, he admired her ardent desire to protect her father's job, even if her efforts were heavy-handed. And she was quite pretty, but he would not allow himself to become attracted to Prudence Willard— not even if she smelled better than a hot apple pie or the fact that he enjoyed seeing her cornflower-blue eyes spark. A trickle of sweat ran down his temple as he continued to stare at her. All manner of expressions crossed her face, and she finally ducked her head, breaking his stare.

"I'm sorry if I said something to upset your sister. It wasn't my intention. I'm far too outspoken—too much like my mother, I'm afraid."

Adam couldn't deny the truth of her comment, but he wouldn't have her believing she'd upset Jenny. "I'm afraid it was the glare I turned on Jenny that sent her running. She's a gentle soul and can't stand thinking she angered or disappointed me."

Prudy cocked her head and looked at him with a placid expression. "Might I ask why she lives with you? She is young and quite pretty. In fact, you two greatly favor one another."

Adam cocked his mouth in an amused grin. "Why, Miss Willard, are you insinuating I'm pretty?"

Her mouth dropped open, and her cheeks flamed. "I. . . uh. . .well. . . You are very handsome, but I wouldn't say you're pretty."

She thought he was handsome? He'd hoped to take some delight in seeing her at a loss for words for once, but she'd shocked *him* speechless. In truth, she was one of the prettiest women he'd ever encountered. Too bad her tongue was as sharp as a new knife. He blinked, trying to regain control of his senses.

"I asked about your sister."

"Yes, well Jenny can tell you her story if she wants, but suffice it to say, she had a bad experience with her intended." He held up his hand when she opened her mouth. "Please don't ask me to share more."

Her lips pinched. "I was only going to say I'm sorry. I believe I can understand a little bit of what she feels."

Adam had heard the story from Prudy's father how she

shamelessly chased after Pastor Parsons before he married Karen. He'd thought it awful how she'd treated Clay's bride-to-be, but he'd never before considered her side of the story. Had Prudy truly loved Clay? Did his marrying Karen hurt her like Jenny had been wounded?

He rubbed the back of his neck. "I would appreciate if you'd not mention to Jenny that I told you about her misfortune. If you two become friends, I'm sure she'll tell you herself."

She smiled and held up her palm. "I promise. I have no desire to hurt her."

"Thank you." Adam glanced at the door. "I would really like to make sure Jenny is all right. Would you mind postponing our discussion?"

Prudy glanced at the clock on the fireplace mantel. "I should be returning home anyway. Mother likes luncheon to be served precisely at noontime." She flashed him a grin. "I will see you tomorrow morning, Mr. Merrick."

Adam's heart sank. Would he have to endure her challenging his every move on a daily basis? "Really, Miss Willard. There's no need for you to be here. I'm perfectly capable of doing the job myself."

"Regardless, I need to protect my father's interests, and that includes this office."

If he hadn't promised Emmett he'd keep things running until he could return to work, Adam might consider walking out and leaving the job to Miss Willard. She sorely tempted him to forget he was a Christian man who believed in turning the other cheek. He sure hoped he wouldn't have to do it every day.

Prudy exited the office with Adam and waited while he locked the door. He bid her good-day and walked away. She watched him go—tall, confident, and handsome. Her heart had nearly burst from her chest when he'd stood close and stared at her for so long. She was used to men staring, so why did it affect her so when he had? He was her adversary, after all.

Spinning on her toes, she headed home, reminding herself what a stubborn, single-minded man Adam Merrick was. She didn't want to like him. She really should stay far away from him, for she feared she could like him much too easily. She hadn't expected him to be so passionate about his duties, and even though she'd treated him harshly, which she could see irritated him, he never lost control of his temper.

With his dark brown hair, deep blue eyes, and tanned skin, he was delightful to look at. She even enjoyed the way his mouth cocked to one side when he had teased her about thinking he was pretty.

Ugh!

She had to stop dwelling on his comeliness and focus on the fact that he could steal her father's job if she wasn't careful. She needed to talk to Papa if he felt up to it after lunch. He had to understand how comfortably Adam

Merrick had settled into his job. Maybe Adam's ideas for making money for the town weren't the best, but he certainly seemed dedicated to the task. She feared he might succeed where her father hadn't—and then the townsfolk might not want her father to return to his job. Her papa had always been so proud to be mayor, and her mother relished in the clout of being the town's first lady. If Papa lost his job permanently they would both be devastated, and she couldn't let that happen.

Chapter 4

After lunch, Prudy carried a tray of hot tea into the parlor of her family home. She'd promised to sit with her papa while her mother ran some errands. Every time she saw him, her heart broke a little more. He'd always been so strong and robust. She remembered delighting in how he would toss her in the air when she was small.

He turned from gazing out the front window and smiled at her. "It's so good to have you home again, Princess."

"I wish I had returned months ago, but. . ." She bit back the words *mother wouldn't let me* and set the tray on a drum table. "It's good to be home."

"I know my sickliness upsets you, but I wish it didn't."

"Really, Papa, how could it not? I want you to regain your health."

He looked toward the window again. "I would like that, too, but I fear it's not meant to be. Still, I've made my peace with God, and it's in His hands now."

Prudy hated that he sounded so resigned. "Don't give up. Please."

He smiled. "There's a big difference in losing hope and resting in the arms of the Savior."

"I do believe I understand that. Aunt Louise helped me to see my need for God." She nibbled her lip and dropped a spoonful of sugar in his tea as she considered the question that had been bothering her for days. There really was no easy way to ask but to just do so. "How will we get by if you're unable to work again?"

He accepted the teacup she held out and took a slow sip. "Sit down, Prudy. There's something I should have told you years ago."

Curious, she plopped onto the edge of a side chair.

With a shaky hand, her father placed the teacup and saucer on the table beside his chair. For a moment, he rested his index fingers against his chin and returned his gaze to her. "We're not as destitute as you may think. Some years ago, I received a substantial inheritance from my uncle Max."

Prudy's eyes widened as she considered the news. "Why have you never told me?"

He grinned. "Because I was afraid you'd want more clothing and froufrous than you already had. You were only nine when he died, and I didn't feel you were old enough to know about financial issues then. I've managed to save the majority of the money so that when I'm gone, you and your mother will have plenty to live on."

There was a huge relief in knowing he'd planned for the future. "I remember Uncle Max. He lived in a mansion in Boston—a very large mansion. Just how well off are we, if I might ask?"

"Well enough that you have no reason to worry about us becoming destitute. And I don't want you pestering Adam about my old job. He's doing a fine job as mayor."

"Interim mayor."

He shook his head, a sad look darkening his gaze. "You have to face the truth, Princess. It's highly unlikely that I will be able to resume that job." He blew out a loud sigh. "I'm not even sure I want to."

"But how can you say that? You lived for that job. I know how important being mayor was to you."

He lifted a brow. "My job was not what I lived for. You and your mother always came first. My job was important because I was able to help the town I grew up in, not because of the prestige."

Things were so different than she'd thought. "But what about Mother? She loves being the matriarch of the town."

"True, but she will be fine as long as she can continue to live in the manner she is accustomed to."

She hated how haughty her mother sounded, but in truth, Helen Willard did see herself as better than others because of their financial status—and to think, it was all because of an inheritance. Prudy's heart clenched. The same could be said about her. She winced as she thought of how horribly she'd treated Karen Parsons when the pastor's fiancée first came to town. She had wanted Clay for herself and had tried to chase Karen away. She needed to apologize, but she was afraid. Bakerstown still had only one church, and all decent women were expected to go to Sunday services. If Karen snubbed her, attending church could be terribly uncomfortable.

A knock at the front door pulled her from her troubling thoughts. "I'll get it. Are you feeling up to having visitors if it's someone to see you, Papa?"

"Yes, but don't let them linger overly long."

She nodded and rushed to answer the door, hoping one of her friends had come to visit. As she pulled it open and saw Pastor Parsons and his wife standing there, she felt the blood drain from her face. Prudy forced a smile. "How nice to see you both again."

Oh dear, she'd just told a falsehood to the preacher.

Pastor Parsons smiled, as did his wife. "We wanted to welcome you back to town and also see how your father is doing."

"I'm sure he's delighted to have you home again, as is your mother," Karen said.

Prudy dared to glance at her and was shamed by the woman's friendly smile. "Thank you. Papa is in the parlor and said he would welcome a short visit."

Pastor Clay removed his hat and escorted his wife inside. Prudy closed the door then led them to the parlor. "Please have a seat. Papa and I were just enjoying some tea. I'll go reheat the water while you visit with him."

"Could I help you?" Karen offered.

Prudy's pulse raced. Did Karen want to get her alone so she could gloat about winning Clay's hand when Prudy had so desperately wanted to marry him at one time? "Uh. . .it really isn't necessary."

Karen's kind smile sparkled in her eyes. "I really don't mind. Now that you're back, I'd like to get to know you better, if you're agreeable to that."

Prudy didn't know what to say. Could the woman be as guileless as she seemed? She glanced at Papa, and he nodded for her to go on. Perhaps he wanted to speak to Pastor Clay alone. "Of course. Just let me get the tray."

In the kitchen, she placed the tray on the table, refilled the teapot, and set it on the stove to heat. With nothing else to do, she forced herself to face Karen. "So, how are you and Pastor getting along?"

"Wonderful!" She beamed and leaned in as if to share a secret. "You probably can't tell yet, but we're expecting our first child."

Prudy blinked, trying to be happy for the couple, but she couldn't help thinking that if she had married Clay, she might now be the one who was carrying his child. A pair of deep blue eyes intruded on her thoughts—Adam Merrick's eyes—but she pushed the troubling thought away. "Oh my, that's. . .um. . .exciting news. Congratulations to you both."

"Thank you." Karen's smile dimmed a little. "I know you

and I had a bit of a rough start when we first met, but I'm hoping we can put it behind us and be friends."

How could she be so forgiving? "I have to admit that you've surprised me. It would well be within your rights to despise me for the deplorable way I treated you."

"I understand that a woman will do almost anything for the man she loves. I'm sorry you were unaware of my relationship with Clay before you fell for him. No one can blame you for something you didn't know about."

Disarmed by the woman's kindness, Prudy leaned back against the counter. "Um. . .I'd like to be friends, too. Thank you. That's very kind of you."

"Don't give it another thought." Karen swatted her hand in the air. "Now that you're home, I hope you'll consider coming to the sewing circle again. I suppose your mother told you that we're meeting at the Spencers' home now."

Prudy nodded. "Mother wrote and told me how she felt it best that she no longer host it, in light of Papa's illness."

"How is he doing, if I might ask?"

Prudy shrugged. "Not nearly as well as I'd hoped."

Karen laid her hand on Prudy's arm. "Your father is a good man. Clay and I have been praying for him."

Tears filled Prudy's eyes. Her mother wouldn't hear of her father not recovering and in some ways seemed oblivious to how ill he actually was. She'd not been able to talk with anyone about her fears, other than crying out to God. A sob slipped out, and Karen wrapped her arms around Prudy.

She wept as all her worries gushed to the surface like an overflowing rain barrel. After a long minute, she stepped back. "I'm sorry. I got your lovely dress wet."

Karen smiled and patted her shoulder. "It will dry." She tucked a strand of Prudy's hair behind her ear. "Please know that if you ever want to talk, you're always welcome at my home."

Fresh tears blurred her vision. "Thank you. I don't deserve your kindness."

"None of us deserves the sacrifice that Jesus made for us in giving His life to set us free from the chains of sin, but He went to the cross anyway. He commands us to love one another. How can I not obey?"

As she lay in bed that night, Prudy wrestled with all that had happened that day. Karen's kindness still astounded her. How could she be so forgiving? She flipped onto her side and stared out the open window. A gentle breeze wafted in, cooling her, and the repetitive chirp of crickets lulled her to a relaxed state. Karen made her want to be a better person. To be more forgiving and less demanding. More like Karen and Aunt Louise and less like her mother. She'd become a Christian while living with Aunt Louise and had grown in her faith, but since she returned to Bakerstown, she had reverted to her old, blustery self.

She yawned. She'd treated Adam Merrick almost as bad as she had Karen. Tomorrow, she needed to apologize.

Chapter 5

Prudy's mother glided into the kitchen. "What's that delicious smell, Betsy?"

Glancing over her shoulder, Prudy smiled. "Good morning, Mother. I talked Betsy into allowing me to bake some dried apple bread."

Her mother shot a scowl at the cook. "It's Betsy's duty to prepare any treats you want, not yours."

Prudy rolled her eyes. "Don't fuss at Betsy, Mother. It was my idea. Besides, how could you be so proud of those awful rhubarb pies I used to make and then fuss at me if I want to do some baking? I learned to cook many things while staying with Aunt Louise."

Her mother motioned for Prudy to follow her. Prudy checked the clock on the shelf—fifteen minutes more before the bread would be finished. She followed her mother to the library, where Helen closed the door.

Crossing her arms, Mother stared at her for a long

moment, making Prudy feel the need to squirm. Had she done something wrong? One thing she hadn't missed while she was gone was being scolded for minor mistakes. "What's wrong?"

"I pay Betsy good money to cook for us. You'll only confuse her if you start assisting her."

"I wasn't helping her. I was making the bread as a gift for someone."

Helen lifted one brow. "For whom?"

Prudy shifted her feet, hoping her mother wouldn't make a mountain out of a molehill. "I was rather rude to Mr. Merrick yesterday, so I'm taking him the bread as part of my apology."

Her mother's gray eyes widened. "You can't do that. Why, he'll think you have designs on him."

"Oh for heaven's sake. He'll think no such thing."

"If you were hard on that man, I'm sure he deserved it."

"You don't like him? Papa seems quite pleased with his efforts."

Helen pointed a finger in her face. "Mark my word, that man is trying to steal your father's job while he is too ill to be aware of the fact."

Prudy scratched her temple. "Why did you invite him and his sister for supper on Friday if you don't like him?"

"I like him fine, but I don't care that he's doing such a good job replacing your father."

"Would you rather he did a bad job?"

Several emotions crossed her mother's face before she narrowed her eyes. "You're trying to trick me, aren't you?"

"No, Mother, I'm not. At first, I was also annoyed that Mr. Merrick was filling Papa's shoes—and his office—but after talking with Papa, I've come to realize he puts his faith in the man doing a decent job and is able to relax, knowing the town is in good hands. If Mr. Merrick fails at his task, then Papa will be sorely disappointed and distressed, so it would be in our best interest to want Mr. Merrick to succeed, don't you think?" Prudy could hardly believe she was defending the man, but she'd realized the truth yesterday afternoon.

After blowing out a loud sigh, her mother relaxed her posture. "I suppose what you say is true." Her hand quivered as she brushed several hairs from her face. "I've almost given up hope that Emmett will ever be able to work again."

Prudy clasped her mother's hand. "Don't give up. Somehow I'll find a way to help Papa get better." But even as she said the words, she knew there was little she could do.

Helen smiled. "Maybe having you home again is just what he needs to rally."

Prudy truly hoped that was the case, but deep down she doubted it.

Adam stood facing his desk, studying a bid to repair the fences at the stockyard. They'd been standing since the railroad came through town nearly two decades ago and were sorely in need of replacing. But doing so would require using up nearly one-third of the town's remaining funds. On the other hand, not repairing them could cause cattle to break free and stampede the town, injuring its citizens and damaging property. Maybe he could ask for bids from other towns, although he hated not giving business to a local carpenter.

A woman glided past his window, and he frowned. It looked like Prudy was going to arrive early today. Lucky him.

As he watched her through another window, she suddenly halted. A man stood directly in front of her. He bent over and smelled something she carried. She took a step backward, and the man followed. Adam rushed to the door. He might not care for Prudy's overpowering ways, but he wouldn't stand by and watch her be harassed by an ill-mannered man. Still, he opened the door and listened to make sure he wasn't jumping to conclusions.

"You sure are pretty, miss. And whatever you're carryin' sure smells toothsome."

"I. . .uh. . . Thank you, but I must be on my way. Please let me pass."

He stepped closer. "What say you and me go somewheres quiet-like and share that delicacy?"

"No. It's a gift for someone. I insist that you let me pass."

Adam had to give Prudy credit for not cowering. The man barely seemed to rattle her. He stepped around the stranger and glanced at Prudy, noticing instant relief when her gaze met his. "Are you all right, Miss Willard?"

"Yes, I believe so. But thank you for coming to check on me."

The dusty cowboy glared at Adam, but he met him gaze for gaze. "We don't like our womenfolk to be pestered on our streets. You'd best tend to your business and be on your way."

"Who are you? The marshal?"

"No, the mayor—and the boxing champion of Briar Glen College for three years running." He stepped in front of Prudy and lifted a brow at the man, issuing a silent challenge.

After a moment, the stranger dropped his gaze to Adam's fist then shrugged. "I didn't mean no harm. Just wanted to yammer with a purty gal."

"That's fine, as long as the gal in question wishes to talk with you. This one doesn't."

The stranger nodded then shuffled back the way he'd come. Adam faced Prudy, whose eyes were wider than normal and emphasized the blue of her irises.

"Is that true?" Her head cocked, eyebrows puckered. "Were you a boxing champion?"

Adam nodded. His manly pride at coming to her rescue wilted a bit, confronted with her disbelief. "I don't need to result to lying to defend your honor, Miss Willard."

She smiled. "I didn't mean to insult you. I was merely curious. And do you suppose we could use our Christian names since we'll be seeing each other frequently?"

Adam stared at her. What happened to the snippety

harpy who'd barged into his office yesterday demanding all manner of information? He searched his mind. Was it possible Prudence Willard had a twin sister?

Her smile drooped. "Would that be such a difficult thing?"

Baffled, he cleared his throat and took a chance this was the same woman. "Uh. . .not at all, uh. . .Prudence. Would you like for me to carry that for you?"

Her smile returned, lifting his spirits with it, and she handed him a plate covered by an embroidered towel. "Thank you, Adam. Now, do you suppose we could go inside? I have something to say that I don't want aired in public."

Down went Adam's spirits. She was putting on an act— being nice while on the street in case anyone was watching. He sighed and stepped back, allowing her to enter first. While her back was turned, he took a whiff of whatever it was he carried, and his stomach gurgled at the delicious aroma.

Prudy removed her hat and gloves, setting them on the corner of Jenny's desk, and then she took the plate from him and also set it down. He'd hoped she'd brought something to share, but perhaps it was for a friend, something he certainly wasn't.

He waited for her to lash out, but this morning she seemed different, less sure of herself. She looked up at him, nibbling her lip, then glanced at the window and back at him. She sucked in a breath and spewed out, "I owe you an apology."

If she'd grown feathers and started squawking, he

wouldn't have been more surprised. The woman who left here yesterday didn't seem like someone who'd ever be so contrite. "For what?"

She threw out her hands. "For everything I've said and done since we first met. I was a nasty shrew yesterday, and for that, I'm sorry."

Dumbfounded, he stood there staring at her. "Are you sure you don't have a twin sister?"

She laughed. "Would you want me to?"

"To be truthful"—he brushed a hand across his cheek—"not if she was like the woman who stormed in here yesterday, but this one, I wouldn't mind so much."

She cocked her head and studied him, probably wondering if he was teasing. "I brought a peace offering." She lifted the towel, folded it, and set it down; then she picked up the plate and held it out to him. A sweet cinnamon scent filled the air, making his mouth water. "I hope you like apple bread."

He grinned. "I hope we argue every week and you feel the need to bring more peace offerings."

Her soft laughter warmed him, making him want to hear that delightful sound over and over. Suddenly she frowned. "Oh bother. I forgot to bring any plates or forks."

"I can help with that. Jenny and I sometimes eat lunch here, so I believe there are a couple we forgot to take home." He opened a cabinet on the wall, removed a pair of plates, and held them out to her. "There are no forks, but these will help a little."

"I apologize for using my fingers. Next time I'll prepare better." She slid a fat slice of apple bread onto one plate then handed it back to him and placed another piece on the other plate. "Is Jenny not coming in today?"

"No, a friend of hers, Patsy Mullins, recently had a baby, and she's helping her."

Prudy gasped. "Patsy is a mother? That's wonderful. So many things change when you're gone for a year and a half."

Adam bit into the bread and closed his eyes, savoring the tantalizing flavors. "Mmm. . . This is amazing, Prudence."

"Prudy, please. Prudence is what my mother calls me, especially when she's angry."

He imagined living with stuffy Helen Willard wasn't easy. The woman reigned over the town, and it had taken him months to get her to leave him alone and let him do things his way. Much like the Prudy who'd been here yesterday, she had tried to run the mayor's office.

"So, have you thought up any new ways to make money for the town?" she asked.

He licked the crumbs from his lips. "As a matter of fact, we may have. What do you think of the idea of a county fair?" Adam took another bite as he watched her mull over the idea.

A slow grin pulled at her lips. "I think that's a wonderful idea. Do you know if any other towns in this county have had one?"

He shook his head. "They haven't. A few host Founder's Day celebrations, but they are small events."

"Are you thinking of something large scale?"

Adam shrugged. "I don't know how big it could be considering the budget. I'm thinking we could have a horse race or two—maybe one for adults and another for older youths. A livestock show and sale. Calf roping and sheep riding for the children."

Prudy frowned. "That sounds more like a rodeo than a fair. What about events for the women?"

He helped himself to a second slice while pondering her question. "What do you have in mind that wouldn't cost much?"

Her eyes brightened as she set her plate down. "The women of Bakerstown pride themselves on their sewing and baking skills." She started pacing. "We could have a quilt show and offer ribbons to the best ones, girls could enter their samplers or sewing projects if we have an event for youth, and we could hold contests for the best pies, jellies, and various canned foods."

"Whoa, there. Where do you think we could hold such an event? No place in town is big enough."

She tapped her finger on her lips, drawing his gaze to them. His gut tightened. This Prudy intrigued him—interested him—but what if she turned back to yesterday's shrew? What could have prompted such a drastic change so quickly?"

"You're not listening." She whacked his arm, making him jump.

He rubbed the spot. "What did I miss? I was thinking."
About you.

"I said we could rent a big tent. My Aunt Louise and I went to a circus held in one last year. I think it's just what we need."

He pursed his lips. "I don't know. . . . I'm afraid we'd have to spend too much money. And we'd need lots of judges."

"Leave the judges to me. As for the money, we could charge a nominal entry fee for each contest with the winner getting a blue ribbon and a small percentage of the total money collected for each event. I'm sure I can get the ladies of the sewing circle to help make ribbons if we need to."

"We'd need tables for most of those events. That would be an expense."

"True." She walked to a window and stared out then pivoted around again, eyes twinkling. "What about asking Pastor Clay if we could use the benches from the church? They would be low, but they just might work."

Adam nodded, catching her vision. "You're right, but we'd have to be mighty careful. Can't you imagine the ruffled feathers if someone bumped into a bench and knocked over a bunch of pies?"

Prudy giggled. "That would be dreadful. Perhaps we need to rethink that plan."

"I agree."

She clapped her hands, her excitement obvious. "This could really work, Adam. With all those events, we could add a lot to the town coffers. We'll have to advertise it though. That's another expense."

"I wonder if we could offer free room and board during the fair for reporters. Say a town's newspaper gives us free advertising, and we put their reporter up in the boardinghouse so they can attend the fair and cover it. That will give us even more exposure and make their readers want to attend next year." He couldn't remember when he'd been so excited.

Prudy laid her hand on his forearm. "That's a brilliant idea."

He glanced down, enjoying her gentle touch, then looked up, capturing her gaze and holding it. His insides simmered, his senses on alert. He hadn't wanted to be attracted to Prudence Willard yesterday, but today, everything had changed. She had changed.

She lowered her eyes and stepped back, a becoming blush staining her cheeks. "It seems we can work together, doesn't it?"

"Indeed." He smiled.

"So, where do we start?"

Chapter 6

Prudy rushed into the mayor's office the next morning, her head swimming with ideas for the county fair. Adam rose from his chair behind the desk when she closed the door.

"Good morning." His deep voice rumbled through the office sending delicious chills up her arms.

She smiled. "Yes, it is." After removing her hat and gloves, she hurried to one of the chairs in front of the desk and sat down. "I told Papa about your idea for a county fair, and he thought it was brilliant. He and I chatted about it all evening, and he gave me some wonderful ideas." Prudy glanced up from scanning the list in her portfolio to see a perplexed expression on Adam's face. "Is something wrong?"

His lips twittered, as if a humorous thought had crossed his mind. "I wasn't sure which Prudy to expect this morning—the sweet, helpful one or the. . .other one."

She lifted a brow. "I do believe I told you that I'm trying

to change my ways. Being around my mother again has made me realize how much I had started acting like her; and I have to say, I don't want to become that woman."

"I'm very relieved to hear that."

She cocked her head, wondering what he really thought of her—and why it mattered. "Was I truly so awful?"

His eyes lifted to the ceiling for a moment. "Maybe unexpected is a better description."

She fought a grin. "I suppose that is fair. I did rather barge in and take over. Again, I apologize for that."

He sat back in his chair. "So, let's hear your ideas."

The door rattled, and Prudy peeked over her shoulder to see Jenny entering. Adam's sister soon joined them, casting Prudy an apprehensive glance. Prudy smiled, hoping to relieve the young woman's concerns.

"We were about to go over the list of ideas that Prudy and her father came up with last night." He looked at her. "Please proceed."

"Concerning the tent, Papa thought we might use the church benches to create a sitting area. We could have a stage at one end of the tent with all of the items to be judged there. People can sit and rest while they view the judging events for the women."

He nodded. "I like that, but we still have the issue of needing tables we don't have."

"There's a sawmill in Sweetgum. I wonder if we could get them to donate the lumber in exchange for some type of free advertising or possibly a complimentary booth?"

"What if we had flyers made announcing the various events and times they will be held?" Jenny said. "Then we could offer free ads to people who help us with donations."

Adam stared at his sister for a long moment then shifted his gaze to Prudy. "I think both ideas are brilliant."

Excitement filled Prudy. "So do I."

"Good. Jenny, do you think you could be in charge of the brochures?"

Her eyes widened but she nodded.

Adam rubbed his jaw. "I'll see about getting the tent and talk to the sawmill owner and some other businessmen who might be able to help. Prudy, could you work on the schedule of events and create short descriptions so we can advertise them in area newspapers?"

"I'd love to. Have you settled on which events you want for the men?"

The next few hours passed quickly as they tossed around ideas and made decisions. Prudy loved the interaction and camaraderie and felt like she had made two new friends. "We have an excellent start. I'm so excited to see how it all plays out."

Jenny nodded. "I sure hope the townsfolk of Bakerstown and the other towns in the county support the fair. It would be dreadful if we did all this work and spent more of the town's money, only to have it flop."

Adam sat with his elbows on his desk, fingers steepled

against his mouth. "It won't," he said with confidence. "People love events that bring them together, give them a chance to see friends and family, and they love to compete. I expect the fair will be a rousing success."

Prudy enjoyed the way his eyes squinted when he smiled. He was so different than she'd first thought. It shamed her that she'd judged Adam Merrick so harshly.

Adam slapped his hands on the desk, making both her and Jenny jump, but his gaze was directed only at her. "What say we go out to lunch and celebrate?"

Prudy nodded. "I'd like that."

Adam was walking in dangerous territory allowing himself to be attracted to Prudy. This sweet, helpful version intrigued him more than a little, and surprisingly, he'd caught himself thinking of her in terms of romance and even marriage. It was crazy since he'd known her less than a week.

If he were honest, he'd have to say the shrewlike Prudence had also caught his interest with her passionate defense of her father's job and insistence on ensuring the town's money and concerns were safe.

He liked that she recognized how she was behaving badly and was working hard to change her ways. So far, he believed she meant what she said. Time would tell, though.

He escorted the ladies, one on each arm, down the empty street toward the small café. Jenny had settled in well to life in the small town, and for that, he was grateful to God. As he listened to the women's chatter, he realized that Prudy and his sister were on their way to becoming friends, and nothing could make him happier.

Adam stood a bit straighter, enjoying having two pretty ladies at his side. He'd often wondered why God had sent him to such a small town. His dreams had been for something loftier, but if God brought him here to find the love of a good woman, well. . .he wouldn't fuss about that.

He smiled as he opened the café door, releasing a barrage of tantalizing smells. He'd prayed so hard to find a way to help the town with its financial crisis, and God had sent him help from a most unlikely source—Prudence Willard. Adam bit his lip to keep from smiling as he seated the ladies. Just think, after the stories he'd heard about Prudy, he'd been half afraid to meet her at the depot.

He dropped into his chair and winked at her, drawing a becoming blush to her cheeks. Yes, sir, God sure had surprised him.

Chapter 7

September 5
Four days before the start of the county fair

As Adam and Prudy walked away from the stockyard, she checked another item off her list. She looped her arm around his and glanced up at him. "I'm really glad Mr. Hampton decided to build another corral at the livery, and that he's willing to let us use it during the fair."

"Me, too. I've had visions of stampeding cattle, with women and children getting hurt."

Prudy lifted one brow, a bit surprised by his comment. Adam didn't seem the type of man to worry so much that it would affect his dreams. In the past few months they'd worked together, he had always been calm, organized, and self-controlled—well, except for the few times she riled him with her stubbornness. "If it makes you feel better, I still have visions of pies on the church benches and someone plopping down on one end, sending them all flying into the air and landing on my mother."

He chuckled. "That might almost be worth seeing."

"Oh!" She spun and smacked him on the arm. "What an awful thing to say. That would be a waste of good pies."

Adam glanced down, his eyes dancing with humor. He pressed her arm against his side. "I'm going to tell her you said that."

She gasped in mock horror. "You'd better not. I'll quit, and you'll have to tend to all the fair details yourself."

His smile drooped. "That would be a nightmare. I don't think I've told you half enough how amazing a job you and Jenny have done. We wouldn't be having this fair without you, Prudy."

She warmed under his praise. "Remember that first day I stormed into your office. I was so certain you were trying to steal Papa's job from him."

"It felt like a cyclone had blown through."

"I'm sorry for that. I suppose I was in a rather stormy mood." As Adam guided her down Main Street, Prudy watched Mr. Lane, the grocer, tack up a row of patriotic bunting, as many of the other business owners had already done. It was a delight to see how excited the whole town was to be hosting the county fair in Bakerstown. "Did I tell you that Mr. Lane told me he's had to reorder sugar and flour and other baking supplies three times in the past month? It would seem the ladies are planning to do their part."

"I'm glad. I've heard plenty of the local farmers and ranchers bragging about their crops and livestock. Each one thinks he has the winning bull or horse. I'm expecting a large turnout."

Adam opened the door of the café, and Prudy entered and sat at an empty table. She flipped back a few pages in her notepad. "On Friday morning, I've arranged with several women to teach classes in ten-yard rag rug making, log cabin quilts, straw hats with decorations, and chair tidies, while the men will be occupied with the livestock sale. After lunch, in the early afternoon, we'll have the first round of horse races and stock horse pulls as well as some of the children's events. Late afternoon will be the preliminary judging for all of the food items and show stock. Then on Friday night, we'll have a square dance and barbecue." She glanced up, hoping he approved of the schedule since it would be hard to change at this late date. "How does that sound?"

He reached across the table and took her hand. "You're an amazing woman, Prudence Willard."

Cheeks flaming, Prudy tugged her hand from his as the waitress rushed toward them. Adam was like no man she'd ever known. Even kindhearted Pastor Clay paled in her eyes when compared to Adam. He made her heart sing and her body tingle with a simple touch or when they shared a private smile. What had started out as a mission to rescue her father's job had turned into an unexpected romance—at least that's how she felt. Was it possible Adam felt the same?

"Prudy? Did you hear the waitress? She asked what you'd like."

"Oh, my apologies. I was thinking. Too many things muddling my mind these days. I'll have a bowl of ham and beans and some lemonade, if you have it."

The waitress nodded, took Adam's order, and then scurried to another table. The delicious aromas made her stomach grumble. She'd been too engrossed in the fair when they entered to notice her hunger.

Adam shook out his napkin and placed it in his lap. "After we eat, I need to make sure the tent crew doesn't need more help. They're going to start erecting it at two."

Prudy's insides swirled. "I can't wait to see it standing. Until that happens, I don't think I'll believe the fair will actually happen."

"Oh, it's happening all right." Adam's look of pride, directed at her, made her sit a bit straighter. "I don't know how you managed to get so many businesses from other towns to come and rent space to advertise their products." He shook his head as if astounded. "A candy maker, Simon & Barnes clothier, a wagon company, and have you seen that water tower going up near the stockyard?"

"Of course I saw it. We were just there."

"So, did everyone come through with the donations for prizes?"

"Yes, surprisingly so. Simon & Barnes donated an overcoat valued at fifteen dollars, which is the prize for the best eight-pound pail of butter exhibited at the fair, and an English worsted suit also valued at fifteen dollars is the prize for whoever wins the horse race. A gunsmith from Independence is coming to show his wares, and he donated a rifle for the winner of the shooting competition. And there are the cash prizes the winners will covet. Jenny is collecting money today from the businesses that are sponsors."

Adam sat back. "I'd say we've done it."

Prudy's mind raced. "Done what?"

"Saved the town's treasury. With all the money we've taken in and will still receive on entry fees, especially since you and Jenny had the foresight to get prizes donated, the town fund is at its highest point ever."

She basked in his praise. "It was a lot of work, but we never could have done it without your help and support."

Embarrassed to receive such a loving gaze from Adam in public, Prudy glanced at her notes. "Oh, did I tell you that several ranchers are going to put on an exhibition of riding tricks for the children on Saturday afternoon while the men play baseball?"

The waitress slid their plates in front of them and spun away.

Adam reached across the table for her hand. Prudy glanced around the crowded café then slid hers into his, hoping no one noticed.

"Lord, thank You for all we've accomplished with Your help. I'm most grateful for this wonderful woman You've brought into my life. We ask Your blessing on this meal. In Jesus' name. Amen." He glanced up, capturing her gaze with his.

Prudy's heart stampeded at the promise in his alluring blue eyes. She didn't tell him her real dreams included him—and a future together.

Adam beamed like a boy with his first knife as Prudy approached the site where the tent was being raised. "The crew foreman is going to let me erect one of the two center poles."

"Are you sure that's safe?"

His brow dipped. "These men put tents up all the time. They know what they're doing."

"True, but you're not experienced like they are." The wind whipped her skirts, causing her to sidestep. Adam reached out, steadying her.

He exhaled a loud sigh. "Have you no faith in me? All I'm doing is holding a pole."

Prudy stepped forward, sorry she'd wounded his manly pride, and touched his arm. "Of course I have faith in you, Adam. I guess I'm a little concerned for your safety."

He cocked his head, a sweet grin tugging at his lips. "Are you worried about me?"

"Didn't I just say that?"

He glanced around then stepped closer and ran his finger down her cheek. "If you're worried about my safety that must mean you have feelings for me, Miss Willard."

She fought a smile. "I wouldn't go that far, Mr. Merrick."

He stared at her for a long moment, and Prudy held his gaze. "Me thinks you doth protest too much." The warm words whispered across her cheek.

"Perhaps." Her grin broke loose, and she shrugged. "A woman does need to keep up appearances. I can hardly wail and gnash my teeth and cry out if you enter that tent before it's securely staked up, can I?"

"Honestly, I have no doubt you could do that, but I'm thankful you have enough self-control not to."

"Mr. Merrick! We're ready for your help." The foreman jogged toward them. He spied Prudy and tipped his hat. "Afternoon, Miss Willard."

"Mr. Andrews. How is the tent-raising coming?"

"Fine and dandy. We're ready to lift the center supports then we'll put up the side poles and tie them down. Should be done in an hour or two."

"Thank you so much for getting the tent here a few days early. I want to have everything prepared and ready to go before the visitors start arriving."

"My pleasure, ma'am." He touched his cap again then punched Adam's arm. "Let's get at it, Mr. Mayor."

Adam's blue eyes flashed with eager anticipation. He squeezed Prudy's hand, flexed his right arm, revealing his bulging muscle, then spun away. She shook her head, chuckling. Behind her rose the excited buzz of conversation, and she turned to see a growing crowd. The tent-raising was something far outside of the ordinary for Bakerstown, and at sixty by one hundred-twenty feet, it would be the biggest structure in town.

The pole on the right was lifted, and the tent rose in the air with it. Right away, the second pole created a point in the top of the tent and rose higher and higher until the left side was even with the right side. Releasing the tense breath she held, Prudy glanced down at her clipboard. She needed to check with Pastor Clay to see when the benches could be moved from the church to the tent. Surely there was no reason it couldn't be done right away since there were no church services until Sunday, and the fair would be over by then. She glanced around again and spied Pastor Clay and Karen strolling toward the crowd and started toward them.

A fierce gust of wind whipped at her skirts and blew a strand of hair across her face. The tent snapped and popped like a hundred sheets on a line. Holding down her skirts, she turned as a loud, unified gasp rose from the crowd. Two men fled the entrance. The tent shuddered, listed to the left, and fell.

"Adam!"

Prudy started forward, but someone grabbed her, holding her back. She looked over her shoulder to see Silas Hightower shake his head.

"You'll only get in the way. Let the men handle things. It ain't the first time this has happened."

Although a bit annoyed, she nodded her head, and he released her. Surely the men trapped would be all right. It's not like the canvas was overly heavy, but could they breathe in there? Her heart clenched at the thought of losing Adam. She thought of him trapped, maybe hurt—she closed her eyes—suffocating. And in that moment she knew—she loved Adam Merrick.

Please, heavenly Father, keep him safe. I can't lose him. Please.

The duo who had raced from the tent returned and were struggling to lift the opening. Men from the crowd rushed forward to help. Together, they lifted up the heavy tent enough to find the opening. Several men set up the poles to keep the side standing while others disappeared inside. On the far side of the tent, bumps lifted and dropped under the canvas, reminding her of when she was a child and her cat crawled under her bedcovers.

Two men hurried out, helping Mr. Andrews. He was on his feet and looked to be all right. He started yelling commands immediately. By her count, at least six more men were still inside. The minutes ticked by tormentingly slow. Why was it taking so long to get everyone out?

Another man crawled out from under the canvas then rose and walked out, fanning himself with a crumpled hat. A man with a bucket jogged up to him, sloshing water. He lifted out a ladle and handed it to the worker. Prudy stared at the opening. Where was Adam? If the other men were fine, surely he was.

Time crept by at the pace of a reluctant schoolboy on his way to the first day of classes. Prudy felt someone near her and glanced over to see Karen standing beside her with Pastor Clay next to her. Karen reached out and squeezed Prudy's hand. "They'll get him out. We're praying."

"Thank you."

A man ran out of the tent, looked around, and yelled, "Someone get the doctor!" He spun and rushed back in.

Heart pounding, Prudy glanced at Karen. The woman stepped closer and wrapped her arm around Prudy's waist. She couldn't stop the trembling in her hands and legs. *Please don't take Adam from me.*

A man appeared, backing out of the tent, carrying another man by the shoulders, while Mr. Andrews held his feet. Prudy stared at the wounded man's light blue shirt—the same light blue as Adam's. *No!*

Her feet pushed into motion, and she hurried forward. They laid him under a tree, and several men crowded around him. "Let me pass. Please. Move!"

The crowd parted. She stopped at Adam's side and dropped to her knees, heedless of propriety. A trickle of blood from a cut on one eyebrow ran down toward his ear. Someone had removed his belt, strapped it around Adam's shoulder and tucked his left arm into it. She glanced up at Mr. Andrews.

"I think his arm is broke," he said. "The big pole fell on him."

"It sure hurts like it's broken," Adam grumbled.

Prudy gasped and jerked her gaze back to Adam's. A pitiful smile pulled at one corner of his mouth. "Howdy, Princess."

She took hold of the hand lying on the ground. "You scared ten years off me. Are you all right? How's your arm? What about your head?"

Eyes shut, he chuckled. "Careful, Princess. You're going to make these good folks think you care for me."

With an air of authority, the doctor forced his way to them and ordered everyone back. Prudy refused to move, even when the man glared at her. She merely glared back. He stooped and examined Adam's head wound and bandaged it, then carefully checked his arm. Adam groaned, and Prudy's heart nearly broke at seeing the man she loved in such pain. In spite of their rocky start, which was mostly her own doing, she'd fallen for Adam Merrick.

Chapter 8

September 10, 1892
County fair, day two

Prudy jumped when the starting gun for the first horse race blasted. The crowd cheered. Riders hooted and kicked their mounts into a quick gallop, stirring up a cloud of dust. She checked the race off her list and looked for Adam. It was time for the final round of the pie judging, for which he'd eagerly volunteered, along with her father, and pie-lover Silas Hightower.

Assuming he was already at the tent, she swung in that direction. All around her, people chatted and laughed. Children ran, squealing and playing impromptu games. She relished the sounds of happiness. Yesterday, the first day of the county fair had gone nearly perfect. More people had signed up for events and contests than they'd dreamed possible. The town treasury had more than quadrupled, and they'd been able to raise the amount of prize money for the winners. Except for the disaster with the tent falling and hurting Adam and a bullet at the shooting competition that ricocheted, breaking a nearby store window, everything had gone smoothly.

On the outskirts of town, she paused where a fat hog was being roasted. The delicious aroma taunted her, reminding her that she'd forgotten to eat lunch. "How's the hog coming, Mr. Poteet?"

He tipped his hat. "Slow and steady, ma'am, but it'll be ready in time for tonight's supper."

"Good. Thank you so much for donating the hog and seeing that it got cooked. I know everyone will enjoy it this evening."

She glanced at her list as she continued to the tent. After the final rounds of judging, all but the three winning pies, which would be returned to the ladies who baked them, would be set out on tonight's food tables, as would all the cakes and sweet breads that had been baked. Never in her wildest dreams could she have imagined so many ladies would want to compete.

With his arm in a crisp, white sling, Adam stood at the entrance to the tent, greeting people as they walked in. Her heart leaped at the sight of him. Who could have dreamed she would find love so quickly upon returning home? Her pulse quickened the closer she got to him. He looked up, sent a special smile directed only to her, then tipped his hat to the man and woman he'd been talking with and walked her way.

"There's my pretty lady."

Blushing like a schoolgirl, she glanced around to see if anyone had overheard. "You're shameless, sir."

"That's not what I'd call it. Overwhelmed by your beauty, amazed with your organizational abilities, and delighted by your sweet demeanor."

Prudy laughed. "I don't know that anyone has referred to me as sweet before, except for maybe my father."

He held out his right arm, and she looped hers through it. "They don't know you as well as I do."

She ducked her head. This man could make her blush faster than the flit of a hummingbird's wing.

He tugged her away from the entrance toward the back of the tent. With no activities in that area, the only people they encountered were a couple of adolescents sparking. The youths stopped suddenly, stared at them wide-eyed, then rushed away in the other direction.

Adam chuckled for a moment then stopped and faced her, all humor fleeing. He studied her face, tucking a strand of hair that had come loose behind her ear. "You're not working too hard, are you?"

She shook her head. "No. I'm having the time of my life. It's so wonderful to see everybody have such fun. What about you? Is your arm hurting?"

"Not too bad. I took a half dose of the powder Doc gave me. It's enough to curb the pain and yet not knock me out." He brushed his knuckles down her cheek. "You're sunburned."

She shrugged. "I took off my straw hat during the three-legged race I ran with Jenny, and then I couldn't find it afterwards."

Adam grinned. "I'll never forget watching that race. You two looked so funny trying to walk with your legs tied together and maneuvering in those long skirts."

Prudy smiled. Seeing him so happy made her happy. "We need to get inside for the pie judging." She cocked her head and sent him a teasing smile. "I know how much you're dreading that."

He straightened and blew out a breath in a self-important manner. "Yes, the things I do for this town. Pure torture."

Prudy giggled.

He sobered and took her hand. "I was going to wait until tonight, but I fear you might be too tired to appreciate the moment."

Her mind swirled. What was he talking about?

His gaze captured hers. "Prudy, this summer has been the best I can remember. Planning the county fair, seeing it all come together, and spending time with you while doing so has been a delight. I almost dread seeing it come to an end."

"There's always next year."

"True. I wish I could hire you as my assistant."

Prudy's hopes dimmed a bit. She'd hoped—prayed that he would soon ask for her hand. But obviously that was not the case. "I'll work for free, Adam. You don't need to hire me."

He stared into her eyes. "What I need, is you at my side—always. Will you marry me, Prudy, and make me the happiest man on earth?"

Prudy gasped. "Do you mean it?"

"With all of my heart." He cupped her cheek, his gaze intense. "I love you and can't stand the thought of being without you. Please, marry me."

Tears blurred her eyes. "Of course I will."

A wide grin split his mouth, and he leaned in, touching his lips to hers. He pulled her close, deepening his kiss and showing her the depth of his love. Far too soon he pulled back and sighed. "I wish I didn't have to judge those pies now."

"Why is that?"

"They'll all taste sour after the sweetness of your lips."

Prudy groaned. "Oh, Adam, that's so droll."

"Too much, huh?" His embarrassed grin warmed her heart.

"Yes, but I love you anyway." She tugged on his shirt, pulling him closer.

Joy engulfed his handsome features, and he pulled her in for another kiss.

"Anyone seen the mayor?" Someone shouted from the far side of the tent.

Prudy giggled. "We really have to go."

"Yes, I believe we do. Come along, my love. There are pies to be judged."

Bestselling author Vickie McDonough grew up wanting to marry a rancher, but instead married a computer geek who is scared of horses. She now lives out her dreams in her fictional stories about ranchers, cowboys, lawmen, and others living in the Old West. Vickie is the award-winning author of thirty-five published books and novellas. Her novels include the fun and feisty Texas Boardinghouse Brides series, and Gabriel's Atonement, Book 1 in her Land Rush Dreams series.

Vickie has been married thirty-nine years to Robert. They have four grown sons, one of whom is married, and a precocious eight-year-old granddaughter. When she's not writing, Vickie enjoys reading, antiquing, watching movies, and traveling. To learn more about Vickie's books or to sign up for her newsletter, visit her website: www.vickiemcdonough.com

THE SUNBONNET BRIDE

BRIDE

by Michelle Ule

Dedicated to:
My favorite businessman and my favorite teacher:
Glenn and Charles Duval
Along with their families:
Bettina, Lynda, Bennett, Elizabeth, Anne,
Catherine, Christopher, and Christina

Chapter 1

Fairhope, Nebraska
Summer 1874

Malcolm MacDougall shook the reigns and peered at the sky late Saturday afternoon. The big draft horses were dancing down the familiar road between Sterling and his hometown of Fairhope, but that was highly unusual. After a long day delivering cargo, they usually plodded home slow, steady, and boring. Today, though, they were in a hurry.

The soggy July heat weighed down on the countryside, and the clouds swirling above looked like fluffy bruises with an odd green tinting the gray. He swallowed a few times, uneasy.

The big Nebraska sky stretched from horizon to horizon, stopping to peek between rustling healthy cornfields of rich emerald green. Gusts of wind shook the tops, waving gold tassels at him. Malcolm frowned. Shouldn't birds have been flying through the corn? Shouldn't he have seen varmints like rabbits and gophers scuttling through the stalks? What had happened to the hum of cicadas?

All he heard was the relatively quick stepping plop of his horses. Something was up and nature knew, God, too. He whistled for his dog.

Sport burst from the cornfield ahead, startling the mahogany horses to a halt. He yipped three times and leaped onto the box seat beside Malcolm, jarring the wagon and nearly knocking Malcolm over.

"Here, there, old boy." Malcolm scratched Sport's ears and tried to calm the shaggy mutt who often looked more like a bedraggled sheep than a dog.

Sport's scratchy pink tongue slurped Malcolm's cheek before he sat. He threw back his head and howled—a long drawn out sound that raised the hair on Malcolm's forearms and set the horses to shuffling.

"Git on, girls," Malcolm called. The clouds scudded way too fast and the light kept shifting from dark to clear. He wrinkled his forehead. Unpredictable weather always bothered him.

Too big to really fear much, Malcolm decided to think on good things rather than those he could not control. Reverend Cummings liked to quote a verse from the Good Book that summed it up well: "Whatsoever things are true, whatsoever things are honest, whatsoever things are just, whatsoever things are pure, whatsoever things are lovely, whatsoever things are of good report; if there be any virtue, and if there be any praise, think on these things."

Problem was that one verse summed up Sally Martin, and her unpredictability unnerved him, too.

Malcolm sighed. The pretty new seamstress in town slipped through life as light as a feather. He could still feel his big hands on her narrow waist as she flew through the air at the last dance. Ewan's fiddle had sung up a fever into Malcolm's bones and made his heart soar. When he danced, his feet moved with a grace he never felt in real life, especially when he partnered Sally.

Wide brown eyes, silky blonde hair, trim little figure, and a wit to match. He knew he was heartsick, but had no idea what to do about it. How did Ewan win his sister Kate's hand?

Music.

Malcolm pursed his lips together and blew a high whistle. Sport sprang to his feet and howled.

He'd have to try something else. Sport's tail shook and he quivered. He barked his alert but happy cry. The horses' ears twitched, and up ahead, coming out of the corn at the end of the field, he saw a kid in patched overalls and his smaller sister. They waved; Malcolm stopped the horses.

"Wind's blowing up fierce, Mr. MacDougall. Can you ride us into town? Pa's sending us to his brother."

Malcolm jerked his head at Sport, who jumped into the back of the empty wagon, tongue out, rear end wagging, joyfully inviting the children to climb in. "No problem, Joe." He reached down to grasp Anna's hand.

Her sunbonnet flapped in a gust of wind, and she folded into fear on the seat beside him. "We'll be there soon," he said. She trembled.

Her twelve-year-old brother pushed back his straw hat. "Looking mighty wild. You thinkin' something might happen?"

Malcolm mopped the back of his neck with his kerchief. "You always got to think funnel cloud on a day like this, but look up ahead. Blue skies over Fairhope."

"Anna don't like the weather. But she does like your Miss Sally."

A warm glow filled Malcolm's gut, but he had to speak the truth. "She's not mine."

"Then why does she smile after you?" Anna asked in a tiny voice.

He cleared his throat over a spurt of pride. "She's friendly; she likes everyone in town."

Anna pulled a handkerchief from her pocket. "She made this for me." The girl traced an embroidered blue letter *A* in the corner. "She's right good with her needle."

"That's why Mrs. Sinclair hired her."

He wondered how long Sally would stay in the small shop on Main Street across from the MacDougall Mercantile. Kate said Sally dreamed of having her own shop. With her skills and cheery disposition, Sally was bound to succeed. She just needed time and capital, but Malcolm couldn't help her there.

"Wind blew down part of our cornfields," Joe said. "Pa thought he saw a twister touch down."

Malcolm urged the horses faster. "Where's he now?"

"Hunkering down near the house. Not enough room in the shelter for all of us, so he said to go to town."

Putting the children into possible danger? Malcolm stared. Thin and wearing patched clothing, Joe and Anna were the oldest of eight children of a sharecropping farmer. If they'd lost corn, the winter could be lean for this family. He frowned. They'd need help.

"You know any songs?" he asked. "I like to sing when I'm afraid."

"You git scared?" Anna whispered.

Only when a pretty girl holds my heart in her hands, he thought, but answered with a nod. "I like to remember God's always with me and I can trust Him. Look, the storm is moving east. We'll be safe in Fairhope."

"Three times three is nine; three times four is twelve; three times five is fifteen." Joe shouted into the blowing wind. Malcolm and Anna echoed his chant.

Ewan had taught him that understanding math meant seeing the pattern. Singing the times tables had helped him. He'd learned to cipher real fine, even multiply and divide; his business thrived now that he could figure the invoices himself.

Learning was a matter of turning your mind to solve a problem. Winning Sally could be like learning math.

Malcolm merely had to figure out the solution to make her love someone.

Someone like him.

Sally Martin knew her latest hat was the envy of all the women in church Sunday morning. Oh, no one said anything, of course; they were all too refined to countenance the sin of envy, but she saw it in their eyes.

Up front her dear friend Kate played a reed flute, accompanying her fiddler husband on "Blest Be the Tie That Binds." "The favorite hymn of a seamstress," Kate had laughed. "You know, tying off the thread?"

Of course she knew. Sally spent her days in front of a newfangled sewing machine or with a needle in hand. She tied knots all day long.

Sally stifled an urge to reach up and knead the base of her neck. After bending over her work all week, she yearned to loosen those muscles, but she couldn't do so here, not in the plain wooden church that brought such comforting worship each Sunday.

She loved her move to Fairhope in May for many reasons, but being able to go to church made her the happiest. She could worship God in an actual church now that she lived in town. Out on the farm a mile from Sterling, her father read the Scriptures on Sunday mornings; they rarely visited with anyone.

But here in Fairhope—Sally glanced about—were far

more interesting possibilities of interaction. Pa had sent her to make a future for herself—and her younger sister. They'd never find husbands on the isolated farm, and he knew it. He was counting on her.

Josiah Finch, the youngest banker in town, tipped his straw hat in her direction.

Sally immediately faced forward. Why wasn't he paying attention to the music?

She looked out of the corner of her eye across the aisle. Malcolm smiled at her then turned red.

"Our hearts in Christian love," sang the congregation. Sally dropped her eyes and tried to hide her answering smile.

Afterward, she hurried outside to join the other women setting up the church potluck. A puff of wind tried to lift her hat. She scanned the horizon. The weather had been unsettled the last couple of days; storms this time of year always worried her.

"Appreciate the prayers, Pastor," said a weathered farmer in his Sunday best. Sally wondered if she should volunteer to let out the straining seams in his cotton shirt.

"Last night's rain should be the last before harvest," Reverend Cummings said. "I just hope it doesn't stir up tornadoes."

"Bad weather went east." He pushed back his hat. "Blue sky's coming our way."

East. Sally looked in the direction of home. Surely they'd

hear if a tornado had set down near Sterling?

"Let me help you." Josiah Finch took the white bowl from her hands. A tall man with piercing blue eyes, he wore a thin goatee under a sharp mustache. Folks thought he looked down his nose at people, but that was only because of his height. His fingernails were always clean, and he smelled of soap. Even on the hot summer day, Josiah tied a ruby cravat under his gray linen suit.

"I'm looking forward to sharing a meal with you today," Josiah said.

Sally nodded, flustered as always at his attention.

"Did you make these pickles yourself?"

She found her tongue. "Kate and I put them up last month. They've been pickling ever since."

"Sweet or dill? Not that it matters; anything you've made will be sweet on my tongue."

"Dill," she said, unsure his remark was proper, especially on Sunday. "Did your mother send a dish?"

His mother seldom left her home, an invalid whom Kate's mother said needed all the sympathy and social contact she could get.

"I brought sarsaparilla. It's what they call a 'soft' drink in Clarkesville."

Josiah had recently returned to Fairhope to help his father with the bank, bringing with him a number of new items from the county seat. He'd showed her *The Ladies Home Journal* and *Women's Home Companion* magazines for his mother, and a surprisingly light bar of hand soap that floated on water.

"What's sarsaparilla taste like?" She stumbled over the name.

He tapped her nose. "You'll have to try it and tell me."

Blushing, Sally hurried to help Mrs. MacDougall, the mercantile owner's wife, with her famous light biscuits. "Have you seen Malcolm?" his mother asked. "I need him to bring the fried chicken from the stove."

"I'll get it." A chore away from Josiah's intimacy could only be good for her.

She pushed open the door to the MacDougall kitchen, only to hear a muffled, "Oomph!"

Sally's fingers went to her lips. She had shoved the door into Malcolm. "I'm sorry. I didn't realize you were here."

He held the platter of fried chicken. "My mother asked me to help."

"She asked me, too." Sally couldn't contain her worry any longer. "What do you think of the weather?"

"Should be fine here. Not so sure about Sterling. How far out of town do your folks live?"

"My father and sister are on the farm, couple miles this side of town. I'm afraid something might have happened to them."

If anyone could help, it would be Malcolm. Big, comfortable, slow-talking Malcolm would have an answer. Not quick like his brother-in-law the schoolteacher, but solid and reliable. When Malcolm said something, you knew it was true.

He gazed at her. Malcolm couldn't always find words, but he danced beautifully. He moved like a hawk in flight, smoothly riding the air currents, but then swooping down at the right moment to spirit away his prey into a heartfelt swing or do-si-do.

Prey? What a silly idea. She felt as safe with Malcolm as she did with his sister Kate. All the MacDougalls were trustworthy folk, willing to help even at inconvenience to themselves. Of course when he looked at her, Sally often felt breathless—and not simply because they danced well together.

"Would you like me to go out and check for you?" Standing there with the chicken platter in hand, Malcolm scarcely looked like a knight in shining armor, but she knew his well-meaning heart, always favorably disposed toward her.

"Thank you, but I expect we'd hear if a tornado touched down."

Malcolm nodded. "Neighbors would send for us. Most tornadoes happen late in the afternoon or early evening anyway."

"No one has come since last night? They're probably fine."

"Will you open the door for me?"

Relief made her giddy. "I'd do anything for you, you know it."

Malcolm stumbled. "Maybe you better carry the chicken. I'm likely to drop it given half a chance."

She laughed and waltzed out the door with him trudging after. She'd just reached the tables when a boy rode up on wild-eyed black stallion lathering at the mouth. "Funnel cloud hit outside of Sterling in the middle of the night," he cried. "We need help. Now!"

Sally turned to Malcolm with stricken eyes.

"I'll take you." Malcolm plunked the platter onto the table. "We'll get Ewan to come, too."

Chapter 2

Debris littered the road and landscape as far as they could see. Crops had been uprooted, tattered leaves lay everywhere, and halfway to Sterling they came upon a wide swath of cropland gashed to the dirt. Ewan veered his horse off the road to follow the tornado-churned field south.

The petite woman beside him shivered. "What do you think?" he asked.

Sally clutched Sport's neck so hard, the dog whimpered. "It headed straight toward home. I hope they're still alive."

He urged his horses forward. "We'll find out."

Bessie and Daisy stepped gingerly off the hard road into the soft field where the wagon wheels turned more slowly. The healthy cornstalks of yesterday were beaten down on either side, the smell of broken corn husks heavy in the air. Sally moaned. "This is the Hulls' field. The crop is lost. What will they do?"

"They're farmers. They'll make do as best they can."

The tornado had destroyed acres of fields. A windmill spun its flag in the distance and Malcolm spied a pile of rubble. "The barn?"

Tears dripped down Sally's cheeks, and she nodded. "What about my family?" Sport licked her cheek.

He put his big hand on her small one and squeezed. She shut her eyes and wept. Malcolm didn't know what to do beyond urge the horses faster and hold her hand. Any other occasion it would have thrilled him, but on that sultry afternoon he meant only comfort.

Folks had already arrived at the Hulls' place. The house had been knocked sideways and they'd have to replace the barn, but the family survived, shaken but unhurt.

Sally rubbed her hands together. "Thank God." She blinked rapidly and stared in the direction of home.

Malcolm prayed they'd find no worse at the Martin farm.

Ewan joined them. "Plenty of helpers here." He met Malcolm's eyes. "I'll ride ahead and meet you at Martin's." He kneed his horse into a gallop.

Malcolm chirruped Bessie and Daisy through the devastated fields.

When they reached the Martin wheat field everything had been turned to straw. Parts of wagons and random tools stuck out of the ground. A rag doll lay face down in a pile of tree branches. Sally whimpered.

"Looked like a good yield," Malcolm observed, then bit his lips shut.

"Pa had big hopes for the crop," Sally said. A windbreak divided the fields from the homestead. Tall trees had been snapped off halfway up with the bark stripped off the north side. When they entered what had been the barnyard, Sally moaned.

The house lay in splintered ruins. A busted wagon rested against the base of the barn—now leaning to its side. Nothing stood upright. Ewan walked among the ruins, scuffing now and then to peer closer at an object.

Bessie and Daisy halted, and Sally jumped from the wagon. Malcolm dismounted and tied off the horses to one of the trees. By the time he turned around, she and Ewan were tossing wood from the house remains.

"We need your strength," Ewan shouted. "There's a beam over the door."

Sally scrubbed at her face but stood back when Malcolm joined them. Sport pawed at the wood. "Storm cellar?" Malcolm asked.

She nodded.

The two men levered the beam off the battered wood cover using a stout branch. They pounded on the door and stood back as it slowly opened out of the earth. The top of a ladder poked up, and Angus Martin followed. He grinned and scrambled out when he saw Sally. "You're alive!" Sally flung her arms around her father's neck.

Her younger sister climbed out behind him and the three clung together.

Malcolm heard a whimper and looked into the shallow hole. A yellow mutt barked and leaped. He reached down and pulled out the family dog.

Angus Martin brushed at his eyes as he surveyed his acreage. "It came on at night, a roar like I never heard before. Filled my ears and near stopped my heart. Didn't think we'd live through it."

Sixteen year-old Lena wept. "What'll we do?"

Martin stepped about his yard looking in all directions. He paused and pointed east. "Some corn is still standing. We're going to be thankful we had stores in the cellar and the land is still here." He turned a bleak face to Malcolm. "You see much damage on your way over?"

"Crops mostly down, but this is only the second place we've come."

"The Hulls are all right, but their barn was destroyed and their house damaged." Sally held Lena and rocked. "I'm so glad you're alive."

"Yep," her father agreed. "Now we'll have to figure out how to rebuild."

Sally stepped among the scattered remains of the family's home. The clock Ma had brought from back east was shattered. The curtains made from gunnysacks were shredded and tossed about the yard. Here and there she spied an unexpected item: an English bone china teacup nestled in a soft pillow; one of her father's boots, Lena's cross-stitch. Little seemed salvageable. She couldn't imagine how they'd manage.

Malcolm found a wooden bucket and filled it at the well. Sally dipped the china cup in the cool water and handed it to her sister—who gulped it down. Her father drank straight from the bucket. "I might as well get used to it. Any sign of my cows?"

Ewan pointed south. "I see something moving."

Ewan climbed onto his horse and with Sport running alongside, trotted off to inspect. Malcolm retrieved the basket of food his mother had pressed on them. He carried blankets and medical supplies in the back, too, along with an ax and other tools. "You hungry?"

They sat in the wagon and munched on the picnic leftovers from Fairhope's church social. "It was dark," Mr. Martin said. "Sky looked like trouble all day. I told Lena we needed to sleep down cellar. We took our bedding and candles and lay among the canned food. When the roaring barreled down and things started flying, I closed the hatch. The wind screeched till we were fair deaf. Worst night I've lived through. It scared me half to death."

"I'm sorry I wasn't here," Sally said.

"Weren't nothing you could have done. I was glad you were safe in Fairhope. You'll stay there."

"I'll come home and help."

"No. Take Lena back with you. You've got a place to stay in town. This farm'll need rebuilding afore womenfolk can live here again. Lena can sew with you."

Sally gathered up the food remains while her father and Malcolm unhitched the horses. The two men planned to ride the countryside looking to help. She and Lena would sort through the ruins.

"When will you be back?" she asked.

Malcolm squinted at the sky. "It'll be nightfall in a couple hours; we'll be back by then. I figure we'll spend the night and see what else needs doing."

"You'll help?"

"You can count on me."

Chapter 3

Bessie and Daisy preferred to work as a team, but could be ridden single. Their broad backs without saddles made riding painful, but in the face of the destruction, Malcolm couldn't complain. They traveled south, following the line of the tornado until they came upon Ewan and Sport staring at the ground.

"Do goats usually give birth in July?" Ewan asked.

Mr. Martin kneeled down. "Old Nanny. Let me help you."

They'd just gotten the tiny kid on his feet nursing when five horsemen rode up. Reverend Cummings led them, with Malcolm's father, Josiah Finch, and two other men from church. All the men looked tired and drawn, though Josiah hardly had a speck of dirt on him.

Malcolm passed a grubby palm across his forehead. The same could not be said of him.

"What have you got?" Da asked.

Malcolm pointed. "New life springs from the rubble."

Reverend Cummings grinned. "Glad one good gift has come of this weather. Other than livestock missing here and there, everyone's accounted for. Plenty of damage, but no loss of life."

"Thank God," Malcolm said.

"Always. Folks will need help to rebuild, though."

"The bank can be of service," Josiah said. "We can loan money against the land."

Malcolm looked at his father. They both knew many of the local farmers relied on credit with the mercantile to get through the year until harvest. Storm damage like this could force many off their land.

"More loans aren't going to help us," Mr. Martin muttered. "Have you seen all my neighbors, then?"

"Looks like the twister gave up about here," Da said. "I reckon one more farmstead and we'll have finished searching this area."

They rode to another farmhouse destroyed by the winds. Malcolm dismounted and joined the men to lift rubble and wood out of the way. Just as at the Martin house, they found another battered storm cellar with the Hulburt family grateful for their release. As the sky cleared toward sunset, the men turned back to the Martin property.

"You're a strong one, aren't you?" Mr. Martin said as he rode Bessie alongside Malcolm on Daisy.

Malcolm shrugged.

"I saw how you got in there and worked. That pretty boy

never got his hands dirty."

Josiah traveled at the front of the group, talking earnestly to Reverend Cummings. When the breeze turned the right way, Malcolm could hear the words: *compound interest rates, security.* The pastor didn't seem impressed.

"Malcolm is good with his hands," Da said. "He can cipher and run his business, valuable skills for Nebraska farmlands."

"My girl speaks well of you. Take care of 'em both for me. I don't know how long it'll take me to make the farm livable."

Malcolm outlined Mr. Martin's plan for his father, who nodded. "A sensible strategy. My wife could use a strong girl to help around the house if Lena needs a job. I'm sure Sally's boardinghouse will make room for the girl in this situation."

"That's what I figure." Mr. Martin shielded the sunset's rays with his hat. "I hope I don't lose it all."

Malcolm patted the kid draped across his horse; the bleating nanny goat trailed behind. "You got a good start to rebuild, and your land's still here."

Mr. Martin stared after Josiah. "Maybe."

Pa said to make Lena sew, to take her mind off what happened, and that's exactly what Sally did when they returned to Fairhope. Welcomed as a refugee by Sally's landlord, Lena was embraced by Fairhope residents, and several brought her clothing and other necessary items. On Tuesday morning at the dressmaker's shop, Sally provided Lena a piece of fresh linen and her box of threads while she got her day's work organized.

The two sat in front of the large window that looked across the dirt street at MacDougall's Mercantile. Sunlight shone in, making the delicate stitching on Mrs. Campbell's new dress easier to see. While Sally hemmed, she tried to find a way to talk to Lena about what had happened. Last night the girl had cried herself to sleep, even though she was thrilled to be in town. While Sterling had a schoolhouse, a blacksmith's shop, and a cramped general store, Fairhope boasted three whole blocks of businesses.

The sweet scent of honeysuckle wafted through the open window. "What was it like?" Sally asked.

Lena shrugged. "The sky looked scary. The wind blew hard. Pa figured we were in for a severe storm, so we took shelter." A ghost of a smile crossed her face. "You should have seen the chickens trying to stand upright. They kept blowing away, so we put them in the hen house."

"Good thinking; it made them easier to find," Sally said. Malcolm had discovered the battered chicken coop a half mile away from the farm; the disgruntled chickens squawking and clucking, but alive.

"My sunbonnet kept trying to blow away, but I tied it tight. It's so clever, the way you shape the brim with reed. You should make more and tell ladies they're twister proof!"

Sally watched her sister playing with the gray silk thread she'd found in the thread box. Lena whipped her hand in a circular fashion, trying to produce a triangular shape. She frowned, shook her head and picked it apart, only to start over.

"What are you doing?" Sally asked.

"Trying to picture what it looked like. Don't funnel clouds start small at the bottom, twisting and turning into a triangular shape?"

"Are you embroidering a tornado?" Sally reached for the linen cloth.

Lena had captured the swirling motion of a funnel cloud with her deft stitches. Sally turned the cloth, marveling at how the threads caught the shimmering light from the window. "You should embroider one of these on your sunbonnet to remember how it stayed put."

Lena picked up her bonnet. "Where should I embroider it?"

This was Sally's specialty: hats. Where would Lena's clever thread picture look best? On the cloth-covered brim, or perhaps on the side where the tie strings attached to the body of the bonnet?

The bell above the door jingled, and Kate entered. She carried soft gauze and wore a shy smile. "Can I hire you to run your machine and hem these?"

Sally raised her eyebrows. "Why?"

Kate giggled. "You're among the first to know. We'll use them as diapers come winter."

The girls squealed together and chattered about the baby to come. After a glance at the clock, Sally set them aside. "I'd be pleased to. The work will be my gift to you."

"Will Mrs. Sinclair allow it?" Kate whispered.

"I'm welcome to use the machine on my own time. Yes."

Lena showed Kate her thread funnel cloud and asked where she thought it belonged on the bonnet.

"What a charming idea. I'd embroider it above the left tie ribbon. It will hide the back of your stitching better there."

Sally turned over the embroidered linen and handed it to Kate. Lena's stitching was so fine, she didn't need to hide the backside.

"It's charming in either spot. I must get back to the mercantile. Thanks!"

They watched her cross the street and pause to talk with a tall man in a pristine jacket.

"Josiah's sure a handsome dandy," Lena said.

He looked in their direction and raised his hand in greeting. Lena waved. Sally felt her face redden and picked up her needle. "Back to work."

They sewed in silence for twenty minutes before Lena held up her olive sunbonnet. "Done."

The clean silver-gray embroidery gleamed against the tired dusty bonnet. Sally bit her lip, trying to figure out why the little funnel shape dressed it up so much.

"This is to show I survived," Lena announced.

The door opened, and Josiah entered. "Welcome to Fairhope, Miss Lena. I extend my condolences on the difficult occasion of your relocation."

Lena ducked her head.

"I trust your father is managing?"

"Yes," Lena murmured.

"Malcolm and Ewan are helping the folks in Sterling. There's a lot of work to do to find their possessions, much less rebuild." Sally looked at the sky out the window. "They hope to bring in what remains of the harvest, too, before another bad storm."

Josiah's brows contracted. "Does your Pa think he'll have a crop to sell this year?"

Sally darted a look at her sister. "He hopes he's got enough food to last until spring planting. The farmers who lost their fields are in a bad way."

"One man's loss is another's opportunity. I hope he fares well. I must return to work. Good day." Josiah tipped his hat and exited. They watched him step carefully down the boardwalk to the bank on the corner.

Lena stared after him. "He doesn't look like he's ever walked behind a plow."

"No. But then, he's never needed to." Sally poked her needle through the cloth and pricked her finger. She stuck it in her mouth.

Financial security was the reward for hard work and often the result of creative activity. Josiah had told her so at the dance, and she meant to prove it in her own life. Sally had plans, and they involved owning a dress shop of her own.

She looked at her sister's newly embroidered bonnet and wondered if it might hold a key to her future.

Maybe.

Chapter 4

Malcolm filled Bessie and Daisy's trough with oats and curried the dust out of their coats as they ate. His muscled ached, and he felt dog tired—Sport already had curled up in a ball near the stall door—but his horses were the key to his livelihood as a teamster for the family mercantile, and they needed care first.

Daisy huffed, and he smiled at her pleasure. The oats even smelled good to him.

The last three days had been exhausting as he'd toiled with Reverend Cummings and others to aid the Sterling farmers. The damage would set back many, including Mr. Martin, by years. He didn't know how they would survive the winter.

Malcolm tightened his jaw. Josiah had been out talking to the farmers, discussing their assets and liabilities. He cringed whenever he saw the polished banker arrive on the scene and while Reverend Cummings had explained the man meant well, Malcolm wasn't so sure.

He was a businessman himself; he understood about profit and loss, but in the midst of catastrophe? Jesus told people to "weep with those who weep." Did they have to lose so much to a tornado and then forfeit whatever they had left to the bank?

Folks needed time to mourn. Later, they could calculate and make the best decision for their families.

Malcolm brushed harder.

He stepped out of the stall as the sun dipped toward the horizon and headed toward Mrs. Sinclair's shop, hoping Sally would be finishing up. Her father had sent him with an assignment.

Sally met him on the boardwalk out front. "Any news? How is Pa?"

"Working hard. He wanted me to give you this." Malcolm handed her a small blue and white cameo.

Her pretty red lips opened in a gasp of joy. "It's not lost! My mother's most precious possession." She showed it to Lena, who clapped her hands.

"When are you going back? Can you take me with you?" Sally asked.

Malcolm hesitated. "I think your pa wants you to stay in town. It's tough living out there without shelter. Once we get all the boards separated out, he'll build a lean-to with what he's got, but it's not a place for womenfolk right now."

"Don't be silly. We lived in a lean-to when we first proved

up the land. I should be helping him. I could cook, if nothing else."

Malcolm lowered his voice. "You need to stay on your job so you'll have income. He's worried about eating this winter."

Sally went still and closed her eyes. Her lips trembled, and Malcolm ached to put his arms around her. But he watched and waited while she processed his words.

"We'll make more sunbonnets," Lena declared. "We can earn money to help Pa that way. See what we've got."

She handed him a green and white checked sunbonnet, cleverly made with a reed frame to keep the sun out of women's eyes. Malcolm had admired the style before—both his mother and sister had bonnets made like this and he'd once cut the thin reed for Sally. Based on his family's experience making reed flutes, he'd shown her how to keep the reed flexible by soaking it in water until she could form it into any shape she wanted.

That had been a good day in the spring sunshine, with the scent of early wildflowers and the shrill calls of fledglings learning to fly. With the dust caked to his clothes and hot skin, Malcolm had a sudden yearning for the cleansing creek waters.

He took a deep breath and attended to the cap in his hand. "What's this?" He traced a triangular shape on the brim, realized how filthy his hands were, and stopped.

"Lena thought it would be memorable to mark the sunbonnet even a tornado couldn't blow off her head. Go ahead and inspect it," she smiled. "It washes."

He turned the creation over, and even his uninformed eye recognized skilled embroidery. "It looks nearly the same on top as on the bottom."

Sally nodded. "My sister is talented."

"You both are. This is real nice. A badge of honor the sunbonnet survived the storm."

"We made two more last night. Perhaps we should give them to women in Sterling whose bonnets did blow away." Sally's shoulders drooped. "How bad is it? I feel so guilty living comfortable in town."

"It's no worse than pioneers deal with everywhere," Malcolm said. "It gives your pa peace of mind knowing you're both safe here."

"I get off on Saturday; will you take me out?" Sally touched his arm, and Malcolm struggled not to react.

"I'll let you know. I scarce know my own business these days."

"Of course." Sally's eyes fell. "I shouldn't presume. We'll see you at the church meeting tonight."

Malcolm watched them walk to their boardinghouse. What meeting?

His mother had filled the hip tub with warm water by the time he entered the house. "Dinner will be in half an hour. I roasted a chicken."

Malcolm could hardly wait.

Scrubbed for the first time in days, Malcolm sat at

the loaded table and stared at the potatoes, greens, and applesauce from last fall. His stomach turned. The good folks of Sterling weren't eating so well and probably wouldn't for months.

He pushed the food around his plate and told his parents what he and Ewan had seen and done.

"Reverend Cummings called a meeting tonight at the church to discuss what more Fairhope can do," his father said. "Are you going back to Sterling tomorrow?"

"Any hauling work needed?"

"A small load when you can get to it out at Brush Creek. Matthew Boden said you should concentrate on those who need help first, but he'd like the goods by the end of the week."

"I'll tell you after the meeting."

Most of the church members were in attendance when they entered the plain wooden building. Kate entertained them before the meeting began by playing her bagpipes—a sound growing on Malcolm, though he knew Ewan still cringed when she played out of tune. Of course, playing out of tune was practically a given with the instrument, but Ewan bore it all cheerfully.

Must be the power of love, Malcolm thought. His eyes drifted across the aisle to where Sally and her sister sat with Josiah and Mr. Finch.

After an opening prayer, Reverend Cummings got straight to the point. "Our brothers and sisters in Sterling are in great need. Several men worked hard this week to help them sort through the ruins. Next week we'll need men to help bring in the harvest. But long term, this winter in particular, will be tough. What can we do?"

Reverend Cummings liked to challenge them, Malcolm mused. He presented a spiritual problem and waited to see how his congregation responded.

"I've been listening to my husband's and brother's stories," Kate said. "We need to raise money to feed them through the winter and buy more seed for next spring. How about a dance? I'm sure Ewan would play and my bagpipes, of course, are always at your disposal."

A good natured groan from Kate's neighbor and a smattering of laughter ran through the congregation. Reverend Cummings looked about the church. "Ewan? You game to play?"

Ewan stood and bowed. "I'm at my wife's service." He looked at her with loving eyes. "Always."

"We could have a pie auction," Kate continued. "All proceeds for the townsfolk of Sterling."

Malcolm figured the congregation would like the idea; most of their social life involved eating.

"My sister can make more of these to sell." Lena jumped to her feet and waved her embroidered sunbonnet. The sharp-eyed deacon's wife behind her leaned in for a closer look.

"Very nice, Sally. I'll take one."

Sally's mouth dropped open and she nodded. "I'd be honored."

Josiah Finch examined the sunbonnet. "I believe this would be of interest to women in Clarkesville. I'll take a sample to town on Tuesday. Perhaps folks from all around, including our county seat, would come for the dance."

The crowd got to work forming committees. Malcolm watched Sally's excited face and thought only one thing.

He wished it had been him, not Josiah, who had volunteered to take one of Sally's sunbonnets to Clarkesville for sale—so the sparkle in her eyes would be aimed at him.

Sally and Lena worked every spare minute to create new sunbonnets. Sewing late into the evenings after work, they devised a system: both cut the fabric from a pattern Sally devised, Sally ran the machine while Lena embroidered. On nights Ewan stayed to help in Sterling, Kate joined them to hem and finish off.

Kate's visits cheered Sally, especially hearing Lena's laughter and enthusiasm when Kate played one of her reed flutes. During the day working alongside Sally, Lena hardly spoke a word. If Sally dropped the heavy sheers or a wagon rumbled past the window, the girl startled and her eyes grew round with fear.

Sally's heart ached with tenderness for her baby sister reliving those awful moments in the dark cellar when the tornado tore apart the only home she knew.

Sally herself trembled if she thought about it too much.

Mrs. Sinclair provided shirts for Lena to hem and other odd jobs while Sally attended her sewing. Spare time previously used to fashion clever hats for the women of Fairhope, she now spent working on the more practical sunbonnets, but the women who stopped in all claimed they'd be purchasing a new one.

"So clever with the framing," Mrs. Fitzgerald said one day. "I don't know how you thought of it."

She passed it to her bosom friend, Mrs. Downdall, who nodded. "Could you make me one in my favorite color: sky blue?"

"A nice color with the dark gray funnel cloud embroidery," Sally said. "And it would look lovely with your features. Do you mind if I sew them after the dance?"

The women agreed and took their leave. They'd purchased a copy of *The Ladies Home Journal* and wanted to read the story together. Sally watched them stroll away arm in arm. She loved Fairhope's friendliness.

Malcolm entered the shop, his large presence filling the room with the smell of horses and sweat. "I'm headed out to see your Pa tomorrow. Do you have anything for him?"

"I'll gather a few things together. When can I go with you?"

He turned his hat in his hands. "I'll ask him. Anything you need?"

She dropped her eyes to the bucket at her feet. "I'm almost out of the reeds I use on the sunbonnet brim. Perhaps if I could go with you on Saturday, we could cut more reeds at Pa's creek?"

His nervous face lighted into a broad grin. "I'd like to take you. But what about Lena?"

Sally bit her lip. "Do you want to come, Lena?"

The girl shook. "Yes. But … but not yet." She rubbed her hand across her face and turned away.

"Kate would probably welcome a visit from you, Lena. Why don't we ask her?"

Sally closed her eyes in relief. She knew Malcolm would fix everything.

The two young women returned to the boardinghouse after work. They ate a small meal and gathered foodstuffs and a fresh blanket for Malcolm to take with him the next morning. Afterward, they sat on the front porch drinking lemonade and stitching.

Josiah stopped at the gate and tipped his hat. Sally invited him to join them.

"I'll get another glass." Lena hastened into the house.

Josiah nestled into her vacated chair, and they sat together in companionable silence. From the pond behind the house, peepers tuned up for a night of song. A lark trilled, and in the distance a dog barked. The neighbor's chickens settled into their coop, and on the table in the window behind Sally, her landlady Mrs. Campbell set a kerosene lamp for light.

"How goes the sewing?" Josiah asked.

She held up the apple-green bonnet made from scraps

she'd scavenged from Mrs. Sinclair's shop. "We've made seven and received orders for four more. I'm pleased."

"You got any here tonight? I'm headed to Clarkesville tomorrow and will show them around town. Kate gave me a poster to put up at the post office in town."

How kind everyone was! Sally dropped her hands into her lap and beamed at Josiah. "I'll send Lena to fetch them and you can choose the best. Perhaps you could take two?"

He stretched out his long legs. He wore a crisp cotton shirt, neatly pressed. His boots were polished and the buckles on his suspenders gleamed. She felt proud sitting next to him where all the townspeople could see.

"I'll take all you've got. They're a good example of your ability and will impress the seamstress over in Clarkesville. It's always good for people to get a sense of your skill when you're in business. You said you want to own a shop one day. What do you like about sewing?" Josiah asked.

"I love the feel of the material and the creativity in putting it together into a garment or hat. I enjoy seeing women walking down the street wearing items I created with my own hands. It gives me satisfaction knowing I made a woman's life prettier and better. Don't you feel the same way about helping people at the bank?"

He shrugged. "You need to make a living with a business. People need clothes, you provide; just make sure you turn a profit so you can stay in business. Most people are undercapitalized and don't always pay attention to where their money goes."

"What do you mean, undercapitalized?"

"I assume you're not in business yet because you don't have enough money to begin."

Sally nodded. "I've been saving, but haven't made much money, so far."

"Do you have an account with our bank? We pay interest on money invested with us." Josiah hooked his thumbs under the suspenders. "If not, come in and I'll open an account for you."

Sally thought of the fifty-seven cents stored in a glass jar under her bed. She knew she'd need much more to begin a business. Calico cost seven cents a yard and cashmere for winter clothing thirty-three cents. A spool of thread could be had for a dime. While she had enough money to make the sunbonnets, nothing else was affordable yet.

"Thank you, but I'm content with my system right now." She said, embarrassed to have him know how little money she had.

Lena returned with a fresh glass of lemonade and promptly retrieved the sunbonnets at Sally's request.

Josiah examined the stitching. "My mother said you can tell the quality of work by how messy the backside is. I can scarce tell the difference."

"Ma taught me how to make invisible knots," Lena said.

"I can see you do excellent work. Which two do you think are your best ones?"

Lena indicated a red-checked sunbonnet and a blue calico. Sally wished she didn't have a pang of misgiving about giving away the bonnets now she knew the cost to make them.

She shook her head. She'd do the right thing even if it cost all the money she had.

Josiah set the bonnets aside and sipped the lemonade. "How's your Pa? Things look mighty difficult out in Sterling."

"He's building a lean-to; Malcolm's helping him."

"I saw MacDougall out there the other day with his grasshopper brother-in-law. He looked as disheveled as ever."

The way he referred to Malcolm and Ewan bothered Sally. "They've given up their time for others."

"Some work with their hands and brawn, others use their brains." Josiah fanned himself with his immaculate straw hat. They sat in a circle of light spilling from the window. The peepers were in full chorus now, and a full moon rose. "He's been building a shack for himself over by his sister and brother-in-law. Imagine, he constructed a barn first for those horses of his."

"Farmers always build the barn first." Sally didn't mean to be short. "They need to take care of the stock. Pa's been searching the countryside for his lost cows."

Josiah sniffed above his precise moustache. "I bet you're happy to be in town. It's much more comfortable here."

"I'll say," Lena agreed.

Sally knew the answer this man expected, but she couldn't

bring herself to speak disloyally about either her father or Malcolm. She looked at her hands. "The people of Fairhope have been very generous. We're excited about the dance. It's good when church people reach out to help others."

"Of course. That's what they're here for." He pulled out a gold pocket watch and frowned. "I must be on my way. I've got to leave early tomorrow for Clarkesville. I hope to have good news for you when I return." He picked up the bonnets. "Good night."

They bade him the same. As he went into the moonlit night, Sally rubbed her hands together and wondered if she really understood town people after all.

Chapter 5

Malcolm helped Sally onto the bench seat and set her picnic basket into his wagon amid the building supplies, rope, hardware, and four cases of canned goods his father sent from the mercantile. Sport leaped in with a yelp.

"Don't you worry about Lena," his mother called, her arm circling the girl's waist. "We'll enjoy our time together. She's going to help me bake before we visit Kate."

Lena waved good-bye as Malcolm climbed onto the seat and called to his horses.

The early morning dawn felt cool as they traveled the well-worn road east. Blackbirds soared through the grasses and into the cornfields on the outskirts of town. One farmer burst through his field waving his hat and shouting at the persnickety birds. Sport agreed with him and barked in greeting.

"Does Pa know I'm coming?" Sally asked.

"He's looking forward to seeing you, but worried about how rough life is on the farm these days, especially after you've grown used to town."

"I'm coming to help, not visit."

Malcolm shrugged. "There's plenty to do. If it weren't for the tornado, where would you prefer to live?"

"I'm better suited for life in town, which is why Pa arranged for me to work for Mrs. Sinclair."

"What do you like about it?"

"You see so few people when you live on a farm. It's one long round of tending the livestock, praying for rain at the right time, and preparing for winter. I want to do more with my life."

"Like what?"

Sally sat up straighter. "Don't you think God created us with unique gifts we should use for his work?"

His shoulders were still stiff from all the hauling he'd been doing the last week. "Yes."

"I like to create with fabric and needle. A town has more folks who can use my talent than a little farm in the country. It's a friendlier place with more people to visit with than on a farm."

"Growing up in the mercantile, I had my fill of seeing people. Driving a rig means I talk with folks all the time. I never thought much about how lonely it might be on a farm, especially for a girl as lively as you," Malcolm said.

She glanced up at him, coloring. "I don't mean to complain. I'll always keep chickens and horses, but I like to make things with my hands rather than grow food. That's all."

Her eyes went dreamy, and Malcolm deliberately turned his head away to watch the road. The angel beside him distracted him too much. He tried to think of another conversation topic.

"Where do you see yourself in the future?" Sally asked.

"Working with Ewan and the mercantile when Da gets too old or Ewan decides not to teach anymore. We're saving our money, and I'm going to buy another team. We'll then do business hauling to the outlying small towns, the places the train will never go, like Sterling."

Malcolm snuck a look at her. "I'd like a wife and family, hopefully a pretty church-going woman who likes town life."

Sally went still. "All you want is beauty, church going, and a woman who likes town living?"

He tugged his hat low over his eyes against the rising sun as they crossed a low hill. "I think marriage is a partnership, a couple working together to make a life. Each is necessary for comfort, encouragement, and entertainment. You're not going to agree on everything, but part of the fun is learning to live together in spite of your differences. You get the basics right, the rest will fall into line."

Sport thrust his head between them, and Sally absently scratched his ears. They traveled in silence.

At a flattened field near where Malcolm had picked up Joe and Anna, he turned off the road toward the ramshackle sod hovel the family called home. The rutted passage bumped him sideways into Sally. "Sorry."

She laughed. "Maybe we should have walked."

A pack of mutts streamed from the fields barking and yipping. Malcolm ordered Sport to stay. The flimsy door opened, and Archibald Owens stepped out, pulling up his dirty suspenders and yawning. "Yer out early, Malcolm."

Joe and several smaller children spilled out from behind him.

"I've brought supplies today. Do you need anything?"

"No way to pay you."

Malcolm had expected his answer. "I've got a case of food to help. How'd your house fare?"

"We'll get by. Unless you got a sack of nails in your wagon and a piece of stovepipe."

Malcolm handed him a three-foot piece of stove pipe and a handful of nails. Owens squinted at him. "I can't pay anything."

"Make sure the children get to school in the fall so Ewan can teach them a new song. Sounds like they know the times tables."

"That right?" He looked at his oldest son.

Joe began to sing the multiplication song.

"He learned them a lot younger than I did." Malcolm shook Owens's hand and climbed up beside Sally.

"I'll do my best to get 'em to school. Pretty odd courting buggy you got there, but I suppose it will do the job." Owens slapped his knee and laughed as they drove out of the yard. The children and dogs ran after the wagon shouting and barking.

Malcolm swallowed and hoped Sally, who had been leaning over her side of the wagon to hand something to Anna, hadn't heard.

Sally bounced against him and grabbed his arm for balance. "Kate told me about you learning math by singing."

He stiffened.

"I'm impressed you stuck with it and learned mathematics well enough to run your own business."

Malcolm could only nod, his tongue too twisted to explain the pleasure he got from turning numbers over in his head now. Ewan had set him to studying geometry and the straight-forward logic of figuring out proofs and angles made long hours on the road go faster. "It pleases me Joe and his brothers and sisters won't learn mathematics as late as I did."

Even as he spoke, he winced. He should be talking to Sally about more romantic things, but maybe it was too early in the morning.

They stopped at the Hull farm where Malcolm off-loaded two cases of food and building supplies. "Thank your father for me," Mr. Hull said. "I'll pass cans along to the neighbors west of here. They're scrambling like the rest of us. Due east, the farms weren't even touched."

"Why would God allow a tornado to destroy one farm and not another?" Sally asked as they drove away.

Malcolm shrugged. "Hard to know why God does the things He does."

Like fixate Malcolm's heart on this pretty girl.

Her father was hoeing the remains of the garden plot when they reached the farm. Sally hugged him and tugged the picnic basket from the wagon. "I've brought you biscuits and a loaf of bread with Mrs. MacDougall's butter and jam."

"A real treat. I've been living on eggs boiled over the fire. Good thing the chickens are still laying."

The men spent the day strengthening and fixing the barn. "I'll live with the animals this winter, but we need to make sure the whole thing won't collapse on me," Pa said.

Sally scrubbed clothes and stretched them over bushes to dry. She inspected her father's food supply and put together a list of items to send out. He'd found the iron stove in the rubble, and she cooked a hot meal.

"Smells mighty fine." Pa rubbed his hands together. "Thank you."

He looked thinner and worry lines crossed his forehead. Sally kissed his cheek. "Maybe you should move to town with us, Pa."

"Who would look after the livestock?" He smacked his lips and forked a piece of fried ham onto his plate.

Sally's heart sank. "I'm sure we could think of something."

"I might have room in my barn, Mr. Martin," Malcolm said.

"I can manage out here for now." Pa waved him off. "You're a good worker, Malcolm. I appreciate all you've done for me and the other folks around here. Not sure I'd be as well off as I am without your help."

"It's about loving your neighbor as yourself." Malcolm's face turned red.

Pa elbowed her. "He doesn't live on the next farm over, but he calls me neighbor."

"Sally works across the street from the mercantile," Malcolm said.

"She's your neighbor, then, not me." Pa laughed.

Pa lay down in the shade for a rest after dinner, but Sally had another need. She led Malcolm down a well-worn path to the creek not far from the homestead, carrying a wooden bucket and a sharp knife.

He rolled up his pant legs and Sally tucked her skirt between her legs and tied it high around her waist. They waded into the slow-moving creek to the green reeds growing along the water's edge, and he filled the bucket with water. "Watch for leeches," she called.

Malcolm grimaced and shuffled in the water to discourage their latching onto his skin.

A friendly breeze blew up, flapping the ends of Sally's bonnet as she scrutinized the green reeds. She called him over, indicating the pliable narrow reeds she wanted.

He fingered them. "How many should I cut?"

"Let's fill the bucket. I don't know when I'll get back out here."

"Are you giving away all the money you make on these sunbonnets to the tornado fund?" Malcolm asked.

"Yes."

"After you pay for the supplies?"

Sally stopped, and the creek water eddied around her knees. "What supplies?"

"Reed is free, but what about the cloth and thread? You can give the cost of supplies to the cause, but no one expects you to go into debt to make them. What would be the point?"

She hadn't considered it that way. Mrs. Sinclair had donated fabric scraps and she'd used her own, but she only had enough free fabric for about a dozen bonnets. "What should I do?"

"Once they sell, pay yourself back the amount you spend on making them and put the rest in the donation box. No one would quarrel with you."

Sally stared at him and licked her lips. Trust Malcolm to see the right answer to a problem she hadn't even anticipated. She took a step closer to him and plunged into an unexpected hole.

Malcolm grabbed for Sally and then tumbled into the water on top of her. They floundered, the heavy skirts tripping Sally, while Malcolm gulped a mouthful of the creek.

When they finally spluttered to shore, Sally laughed at the water streaming down Malcolm's face. "Look how well my reed brim kept its shape." Her clothes were a soggy mess, but the brim shielded the water from dripping into her eyes. "Thank you for saving me."

"That's a might clever bonnet you got there." Malcolm took a deep breath, leaned in, and kissed her, sweet and gentle.

"Where are you?" Pa shouted from the knoll above.

Malcolm spun away, slipped, and floundered in the current.

Pa climbed down the path, reached the creek bank, and put his hands on his hips. "You may be a man of action and few words, Malcolm, but surely you know better than to fall in." He reached for Sally with a frown. "You better stay away from him until your clothes dry off."

Sally put her fingers to her lips and watched Malcolm float around a bend in the creek. Despite the clingy, wet clothes her cheeks flared hot, and she wondered what else Malcolm knew that she had not anticipated.

A man of action and few words, indeed!

Chapter 6

Helping Sally cut reeds reminded Malcolm of his childhood and the reed flutes he'd made with Kate and Ewan. Ewan had taught the Fairhope school children how to make and play reed flutes last Christmas; you could still hear them piping around town.

But the Sterling children didn't know about reed flutes and the joy of making music.

He'd watched Lena shake when asked about the tornado, but he'd also seen her face light up when Kate blew her ridiculous bagpipes. Music might help calm Lena's jittery soul.

Malcolm decided to find out.

He visited the Martin sisters sitting on the front porch after supper Monday night.

Dusk came, and the first bats flickered in the dying light. Playing children shouted down the street, and the heavy scent of honeysuckle hung in the air. Mrs. Campbell waved at him after she set the kerosene lamp in the window.

"What's in the bag?" Lena craned her neck and sat taller on her chair.

"A present for you." He brought out two reed flutes. The teenager's eyes grew wide, and she set aside her embroidery. "One for you and one for me."

He looked at Sally. "Did you want one, too?"

Her eyes gleamed, and she shook her head. "Thank you for thinking of Lena."

Malcolm demonstrated how to cover the holes with his fingers and blew. He played up the scale, nowhere near as clearly as his sister, but good enough to satisfy.

He'd already taught Lena to play "Twinkle, Twinkle, Little Star" when Kate and Ewan joined them.

"Sweet piping!" Kate called. She took the flute from her brother and blew. "It's new, but has a nice tone. What are you up to?"

He looked at Ewan, who clapped him on the back. "He's seen the kids out in Sterling who've lost everything and thought he'd make them a gift, right?"

Malcolm nodded.

"I'm proud to call you my brother. Your heart is good, like the preacher says, and you let those little children come to you."

"Thinking about their need, that's all."

Kate hugged him. "God often reveals himself best in the little things. We're going to Ma and Da's house for ice cream. They've got one of those new crank machines and a little bit left of last winter's ice. Would you like to join us?" She extended the invitation to all.

Lena jumped up. "I would."

"Your embroidery?" Sally asked.

"I'll take it with me—Mrs. MacDougall won't mind."

"I'll be there in a bit," Malcolm said.

The three strolled away while Sally bent her head over the latest sunbonnet, this one in navy blue with red strings.

"The reeds work all right?" Malcolm asked.

She nodded and licked her lips, seemingly intent on what she was doing. "How did you know she needed a flute to cheer her up?"

"It seemed like the right thing to do," Malcolm finally said, desperate to say something about his feelings, but unsure of her reaction. He scratched at a mark on the porch. "I'd do anything for you, Sally."

She opened her mouth to reply when Josiah's voice rang out. "I've found you! I've got great news from Clarkesville."

"I'll be on my way, then," Malcolm said. "Ice cream."

Sally's heart sank as Malcolm shuffled down the street, but she put a pert smile on her face and indicated the empty chair opposite. Josiah removed his jacket and sat. "Pleasant out here, isn't it?"

Actually, the mosquitoes were buzzing, and the humidity meant she dripped sweat. The MacDougall ice cream sounded refreshing, but she'd missed her chance. Sally pushed back her hair. "How was your day?"

"Very profitable for you. The shop owner I saw in Clarkesville fell in love with your bonnets. She sold one while I stood there and asked me to bring more."

Sally rubbed her hands on the cotton fabric in her lap. "They're just bonnets."

"Apparently the woman who bought one appreciated that the brim didn't droop. She loved the idea of helping victims by purchasing one. You could easily sell a dozen." He pulled six bits from his pocket. "Here's your pay for two bonnets."

"Thirty-seven cents. It's a good start."

"Would you like to open a bank account with this?" Josiah tapped his index finger on the coins.

"No. I'm going to turn it over to Reverend Cummings. It doesn't belong to me."

"You should deduct the costs. You shouldn't go into debt trying to help people."

Malcolm had said the same thing. Sally shifted in her cane back chair. She understood the reason, now, but it still didn't seem quite right to her.

"There's nothing wrong with turning a small profit," Josiah said. "If this gets you started with the Clarkesville ladies, you could sew other clever hats and the like. This could be your foot in the door. Why not sell there?"

"We'll see how many I have left after the dance on

Saturday. You could take those to Clarkesville next time you go."

He stretched his hands behind his head. "You may sell out in Fairhope. Then what will you do?"

Light spilled from the house across the street, and she heard friendly laughter. "I'll be thankful God heard our prayers for those in need, which includes my father."

His eyes danced. "Are you thinking like a business woman or a do-gooder?"

She knew the answer he sought, but she felt uncomfortable holding back some of the money received for the bonnets. There was so much Sally needed to learn about business before she could open her own shop. A banker could advise and help her. He knew all about money and interest rates.

Josiah spoke slowly. "Profits are one thing; if you don't feel comfortable keeping the profit, don't. But the material costs are something else. Good business sense isn't greed. By managing your resources you'll ensure you can keep on making sunbonnets and thus help those in need."

Sally bit her lip, trying to think of a good response. "Why can't I be both a seamstress who turns out quality work and provides for those in need; you know like the Proverbs 31 woman?"

Josiah closed his eyes. "Is she the one known for being worth more than rubies and pearls?"

"Yes, 'she reacheth forth her hands to the needy' and 'she maketh herself coverings of tapestry, her clothing is silk and purple.' She's very resourceful."

"As are you. I work hard for the same reason," Josiah said. "I want to make a life for my family and clothe my wife in silk and purple. How's that sound?"

Sally thought of the way cool silk slipped through her fingers when she'd had opportunity to stitch it. "Any woman married to you would have a comfortable life."

"My father gave me a parcel of land outside of town where I'm going to build a house. The bank will be mine one day. I'm thinking an elegant two-story with a wrap-around porch and scroll work. It'll include four bedrooms upstairs and a deep cellar beneath. Would a house like that appeal to you?"

Her father's lean-to flashed in Sally's mind, along with gratitude for the cellar that sheltered him and Lena during the tornado. "In this area a storm cellar is a good idea. It saved Pa and Lena's lives."

"I drove out there to survey the damage before I went to Clarkesville. Many of those folks are pressed to the wall. We're offering them reduced interest on any loans they take out against their land, but some farmers may go under."

Josiah looked at her and stopped. Sally couldn't keep the horror off her face. "You would take advantage of people in this situation?"

"Not at all. We're offering lower rates. A small loan could help them keep their land until they get a good crop or they can sell."

She rubbed her face and thought of Malcolm's hands dirty from working for her father and his neighbors. He had asked for nothing in return. Sally glared at Josiah. "Did you ride your horse or buggy?"

"I took my horse; the roads are chewed up and hard on the buggy."

"So you took no provisions with you? No extra food? No building supplies? Did you even get your hands dirty?"

He frowned. "No need. I carried paperwork in my saddlebags. It takes all kinds of people to help. The Good Book reminds us the body is made up of many members. Some are teachers, some are workers, and some are leaders."

Josiah scratched the back of his head, frustrated. "What good would it do for me to build a barn if I don't know how? I'd be in the way. We've been busy at the bank making sure we have the funds to help. My skills lie in using my brains, not my brawn."

Josiah could add up a column of numbers faster than anyone she knew. He understood how the world outside of Fairhope worked and wanted to do the right thing. She doubted he could pound a nail straight. Drumming up sales for her bonnets and seeking ways to reduce the financial burden on farmers was important.

Sally took a deep breath of the warm evening air and thought of Malcolm's cheerful and strong helpfulness. She wished Josiah's clean hands and suit didn't feel like shirking to her.

Chapter 7

Malcolm woke early the morning of the fund-raising dance. The heat had modulated and he had work of his own to do. He started with the most important task: finishing a dozen reed flutes for the children of Sterling.

Kate thought they'd make these flutes different from their normal ones. She'd painted them red and then decorated the front with a twister shape. "Sort of like what Lena did with the bonnets."

Once they dried, Malcolm sanded the bottoms and carved finger holes. He tested each one in turn to make sure it wasn't difficult to blow. They looked pretty and should cheer up the children.

Afterward, he cleaned his wagon and harness, brushed Bessie and Daisy, threw sticks for Sport to chase, and sat on a bench to think. He even prayed for wisdom and was still resting in the shade when Ewan came looking for him.

"It's a big day today." Ewan leaned against the ash tree beside the MacDougall house. "What are you going to do?"

Malcolm frowned. "I'll go to the prayer meeting at three o'clock, then attend the auction and bid on a pie. I expect I'll dance while you play." He sighed. "I'll enjoy dancing again. Feels like I've done nothing but work since the tornado came through."

"What are you going to do about Sally? While you've been tongue-tied and quiet, Josiah's been courting her. He's been describing a big house he's going to build and the fine clothes he'll buy for his wife and family."

The peace Malcolm thought he'd found evaporated and his guts clenched.

Overhead a mockingbird called, its trilling voice starting high and sweet and descending into a noise that sounded like a whining dog. Both men looked up, and Sport ran into the yard, barking to match, spinning around looking for a strange animal, and finally collapsing against Malcolm's leg in confusion.

"While he explored the neighborhood," Ewan said, "a nosey bird landed in his yard and stole his voice."

"What's your point?" Malcolm had to push the words past a tight throat.

"Josiah's not a bad guy. He's lonely and is attracted to a pretty girl. He's a smooth talker and has a lot to offer." Ewan picked up a stick and threw it for Sport to chase. "I'm saying I think Sally has more in common with you than Josiah, and you could make her happier. Don't let her fly off with a wealthy bird."

Malcolm could feel his ears turning red. He'd never been as quick of tongue or clever as his sister or Ewan. What he knew to do was work, and to work hard. Surely Sally had recognized his affection for her through his actions?

Ewan watched him through steady eyes. "Put your mouth in front of your muscle. Offer your heart to her. I'd pray, too. In fact, I will pray."

Malcolm had been praying about what to say to her, and then his brother-in-law came over warning him to speak up. His heart sank.

"Maybe she'd be better off with Josiah. He can give her all the things she wants, a beautiful home and clothes."

Ewan tossed the stick again. "I told myself the same thing when he tried to court Kate. But what kind of man throws away the love of a good woman because he's afraid of being rejected? Give her the choice, Malcolm. Right now, all she sees is one man interested, and he's dangling security."

Malcolm squeezed his big hands together trying not to shake at Ewan's forcefulness. He meant well. He'd taught Malcolm how to solve seemingly insurmountable math problems.

But music and singing couldn't help him past this problem. This required more action than words, Malcolm knew. If only they could dance or work together. How could he demonstrate his feelings to Sally and his hope for a future with her?

Dance?

Pie auction?

"They were baking pies when I went by the boarding house," Ewan said. "Lena was pitting cherries on the front porch."

Sport returned with his stick, and Malcolm scratched the dog's ears. "Thanks."

Prayer comforted and encouraged her every time, Sally thought as she exited the church with the dozens of folks who had gathered. Pa had come in early from Sterling. He nudged her. "Proud to be here in my new shirt to ask God for mercy and help."

She'd stayed up late the night before finishing it, along with completing the last of the dozen sunbonnets. Up since dawn, Sally felt lethargic on the warm day. She'd need to muster energy for tonight's dance. The auction's excitement should help.

Pa shook hands with Josiah, who tipped his hat in her direction. "Will you give me a hint?" Josiah asked.

"Gingham ribbon," Lena said.

Sally whirled on her. "You're not supposed to give hints of what pie is yours."

"Thank you, kindly. I'll be watching for it. How goes the rebuilding, sir?"

Pa eyed him. "I'll be able to winter over. I'm thankful my girls have a place in town."

"Your family will always be welcome here."

"Will your mother join us today?" Sally asked. She'd never laid eyes on his mother, though his father would be conducting the auction in a short time.

"Alas, no. She never goes out." He touched her cheek. "I'll see you soon."

He hustled out of the church.

"He's mighty forward," Pa said. "He courtin' you without my permission?"

"Pa."

"He likes her, but she likes Malcolm better," Lena said.

"Shh."

"Better choice," Pa grunted.

Sally glanced about to see if anyone heard. Her chest felt tight and her stomach roiled. She wanted to rub Josiah's touch off her cheek and lean against someone strong and immovable, a man to hold her up and encourage her. She had felt reassured when Malcolm's deep voice had prayed not twenty minutes before. Where was he now?

"What kind of pie did you make for me?" Pa asked Lena.

She batted her lashes. "You'll find your favorite on the table."

Outside the church, people hurried to finish organizing tables of goods and pies for auction. Mr. Finch shouted for their attention.

People must have come from all around the county, including well-dressed folks Sally suspected journeyed from Clarkesville. The livery stable was full of extra horses and buggies. Josiah greeted several and motioned for her to join him. Sally shook her head and hurried to assist Kate whose arms were full of plates.

"Quite a turnout. Did you see that Clarkesville woman's hat?" Kate ducked her head in the direction of an elegant woman in a fine poke bonnet.

Sally told herself not to stare, but she wanted to inspect how the hat had been constructed. A hatter had woven reeds to create the shape and adorned it with silk flowers. She'd try to create a similar style when she got a chance.

Her landlady joined them, shaking her fine skirts and spinning with pleasure. The hoops she wore belled out the new dress beautifully, and Mrs. Campbell preened with rosy cheeks and a spring in her step. "I'm going to try for one of your bonnets, Sally. I've enjoyed watching you and Lena make them on my front porch."

"Thank you for providing the lamp for us to work."

Rev. Cummings joined Mr. Finch and called the excited crowd to order. They bent their heads and prayed for God's blessings on their day, reminding Him the purpose was to provide relief to their brothers and sisters in Sterling.

"Amen," Sally whispered, as a curious thrumming grew inside her heart. This day could change her family's fortunes from grim to hopeful. She had to trust God to provide the means to deliver them, even though Pa thought he could winter over successfully in the barn with his animals.

Sally hoped for better options.

She looked around the churchyard. Where was Malcolm?

Mr. MacDougall handed Mr. Finch an auctioneer's gavel and he hammered it onto the podium brought from the church. "Let the auction begin!"

Chapter 8

Malcolm stood in the back of the crowd, watching as Mr. Finch auctioned off livestock. A cheer went up from the crowd when the livery agent passed the hearty banker a note. "Charlie Grech from the north side of Fairhope announces he's got more laying hens than he knows what to do with. He'll give one layer to each of the first ten Sterling families who find him."

A spirited bidding broke out when five jars of his mother's wild blackberry preserves went up on the auction block. They sold for two bits each. Ma blushed until she saw the winner: his father. "I'm not letting these preserves out of my house if I can help it!" Da shouted.

Laughter.

The spirited crowd obviously enjoyed themselves, but Malcolm couldn't join in. He kept his eyes on Sally, who scanned the crowd and twisted her handkerchief. He couldn't make sense of it; Josiah stood nearby and obviously sought her attention. Still she looked, and he scanned the crowd with her, for what he didn't know.

Children ran about with a freedom Malcolm envied. Even Joe and Anna, along with their siblings, seemed lighthearted. A mockingbird in a nearby tree, maybe the same one from earlier, coughed a sound similar to the auctioneer's gavel. It felt like the whole world was making fun of him.

"Miss Sally Martin needs to come forward to model this fine bonnet," Mr. Finch called. "A beautiful girl wearing a beautiful hat. Who can resist?"

Not Malcolm. He paced. Perhaps he could buy one for Kate or his mother? He still hadn't come up with an idea yet as to how to win Sally's hand, but this seemed to be the day.

Kate needed a green hat with her hair color, so he let the first two bonnets go by. On the third choice, however, he realized a murmur had begun as the price, once more, went to five bits. It seemed a reasonable price to Malcolm. He didn't understand the restlessness.

The fourth choice, a sky blue model; the fifth and sixth, both made of blue calico; all went for five bits, though the seventh yellow bonnet went for seven.

Ewan appeared at his elbow. "What do you think he's up to?"
"Who?"

"Haven't you noticed? Josiah's bought them all. He hasn't got seven heads to wear a bonnet on, and everyone knows his mother never goes outdoors. Who's he buying them for?"

Sally didn't look so merry anymore as she modeled

a green checked bonnet. Malcolm raised his hand to bid. "Eight bits," he shouted.

People turned in his direction.

Josiah went to ten.

While Malcolm fumbled in his pockets checking his money, the gavel came down hard. Sold.

And so it went. Josiah bought all twelve bonnets.

Sally climbed down from the chair, her face downcast and red. She nodded at Josiah and then hurried into the mercantile with Kate following close behind.

"What is he thinking?" Sally burst into tears. "Why would he buy all those bonnets? It's presumptuous and humiliating and"—her eyes widened—"what will people think?" *What will Malcolm think?*

Kate stretched out her arms. Sally went to her, and they hugged each other. "I'm sure he's got a clever reason; he never acts impulsively. Let's be thankful for how much money your bonnets raised for the fund."

"I can't go out there. People will think I put him up to it. They'll think. . . I don't even know." Sally looked into Kate's sympathetic eyes. "They'll think he's courting me, won't they?"

"Isn't he?"

"I don't know," she wailed. "I just wish someone else had bought a sunbonnet."

The bell jingled above the door, and Malcolm entered. "Is Sally okay?"

She buried her face into Kate's shoulder. She couldn't look at him.

"I'll take care of her," Kate said. Sally felt Kate motion to shoo him away.

"Would you like me to punch him in the nose, Sally?"

Trust Malcolm to make her feel better. "No!" She laughed in spite of herself. "But thank you."

"They'll be bidding on the pies soon," he said. "I'll see you then." He shut the door with a click, and the mercantile went silent.

Kate rubbed Sally's arm. "What do you want to do?"

She felt wrung out. "Find out who's won my pie. It's wrapped in a plain white pillow slip with a sunflower on top."

They returned to the auction, where Mr. Finch had just announced Rev. Cummings as the winner of the suckling pig. "Raise him up and you could have bacon next year."

The reverend's daughter Grace began to cry. "I don't want to kill the piggy."

A murmur of sympathy moved through the crowd. Grace carried the pink creature to her spinster aunt who frowned at her brother and took her niece and the piglet home.

"Here's a novel item you don't see very often." Mr. Finch fumbled with a collapsing pile of sticks and bellows.

"Hey," Kate cried. "What are you doing with my bagpipes?"

He pretended innocence. "These are yours? They came from an anonymous donor."

Kate put her hands on her hips and looked about the

people gathered around him. "All I can say is the donor better be bidding."

Ewan sheepishly handed Mr. Finch a silver dollar. "We need to keep harmony in the family, whether this instrument will provide it or not."

The congregation roared. "Won't you play a little song, Mrs. Murray, to entertain us while we get the pie auction organized?"

"Thank you, Mr. Finch. I'd be glad to." Kate stepped up, adjusted her instrument, blew hard into the bellows to engage the low drone, and played a fair representation of "Amazing Grace."

"She sounds much improved." Sally said to Mrs. MacDougall. The woman had proud tears in her eyes.

"She's been practicing. My Kate's a determined young woman, as you know." Mrs. MacDougall darted a look at Sally. "And my Malcolm is a fine and honorable man."

"I know," Sally whispered. "He's a problem solver and so steady and helpful. I feel safe when I bring a concern to him."

"Mark my words. When Malcolm loves, he loves deeply. Don't break his heart." Mrs. MacDougall hurried to help with the pies.

Sally's mouth dropped open in surprise, while the thrumming grew stronger in her chest. Could Mrs. MacDougall be right? She surveyed the crowd, suddenly anxious. What had become of Malcolm?

Chapter 9

Malcolm returned to the back of the crowd after helping Grace Cummings find a spot in the family barn for her piglet, which she had named Hamlet.

His mother held aloft the first item as Mr. Finch extolled the virtues of a cherry pie with a red gingham bow. The young man who ran the livery stable started things hopping when he shouted "four bits."

Josiah jumped in with five while a man in a white hat from Clarkesville bellowed six. "I haven't tasted a good cherry pie in years."

Mr. Martin bid seven, but Josiah's ten silenced him. Malcolm pulled the coins from his pocket. He had two silver dollars to spare. He shouted them out.

The crowd silenced, and then Josiah raised him. No one said a word, the gavel came down, and the fine cherry pie went to the young banker.

Malcolm set his jaw and blinked several times, tightening

his fists and wishing he'd saved more than two dollars. He heard children playing by the creek and picked up his bag of flutes. Time to swallow his own disappointment and pass them out to those who needed encouragement.

Eight children swarmed him when he reached the creek. Two knew exactly what to do and began piping immediately. The rest needed help to spread their fingers across the holes and a demonstration on how to play. Their excitement made Malcolm's sore heart lighten.

One boy attended Ewan's class and tried to teach them how to play the school's signature tune, 'Joy to the World.' Malcolm sat on a rock watching until his sister hustled up.

"What are you doing? Get up there. Her pie is nearly the last one to be auctioned."

"Who's pie? I only wanted Sally's."

"Exactly. Sally's pie is in a white cloth with a sunflower on top."

"I thought she made a cherry pie with a gingham ribbon."

Kate laughed. "No. You should have seen Josiah's face when Lena took his arm. She made the cherry pie, not Sally."

Malcolm ran back to the church, just as Mr. Finch raised his gavel on two bits.

"A silver dollar," Malcolm shouted.

Josiah glowered at him, Sally stood tall and smiled, and Mr. Finch brought down the gavel. "Eight bits. You've won yourself a wild blackberry pie, Mr. MacDougall."

Behind him, Ewan pretended to faint in relief.

Sally's rosy face beamed as she approached him. "Thank you for not letting me be embarrassed," she whispered. "Old Man Reynolds was the only bidder."

Malcolm looked to where the crippled farmer slumped against a cottonwood tree. "Let's share a piece with him."

So giddy at winning the pie, Malcolm gave half of it to the eighty-year-old bachelor.

"Thank you, Malcolm," he said. "You've always been a generous young man."

They joined Lena and Josiah at a table. His teeth were red from the cherry juice, and he growled a greeting.

Lena cut him another piece, her face a wreath of happiness.

"Why did you buy all my bonnets?" Sally asked.

"Purely a business proposition. The Clarkesville haberdasher asked me to buy them. The Sterling fund makes money, and I'll turn a little profit selling them to him. He, obviously, expects to do the same. I told you, these bonnets can be a foot in the door for selling your creations in Clarkesville."

Sally picked up her wild blackberry pie pan. "How dare you?"

"What do you mean? I've marketed your creation. All sorts of women will want you to sew for them after this. These bonnets can be a good start to the business you said you wanted."

Sally put one fist on her hip and leaned toward him. "Are you going to put your 'profit' into the funds box?"

Josiah put up his hands. "I've already contributed plenty by buying them in the first place."

Malcolm stirred. He didn't like how she balanced the

remains of his pie on her fingertips. "Let me take the rest of the pie. I haven't had a slice yet."

Joe, Anna, and their younger siblings burst into the area before the church, piping shrill whistles on their flutes. Several Fairhope children ran off to get their flutes, and before long "Joy to the World" rang in the square.

Kate stepped forward to shout over the noise. "The dance is about to start. Finish your pie!"

Malcolm lunged for his.

"I didn't mean for it to slip like that." Sally stared at the blackberry mess in Josiah's lap.

He sputtered and shoved back his chair, nearly upending it. Lena ran for a cloth.

"I'm so sorry, Josiah," Sally began.

Malcolm's dog Sport lapped at the juice.

Malcolm slumped. "My pie."

"I would have given you everything you ever wanted," Josiah sputtered. "Beautiful silk clothing, a house, a buggy. With my business savvy and your creativity, we could have built your business together. But you never appreciated my efforts. Every time I tried to get close, Malcolm was there, worming his way into your affections. What type of man do you really want?"

She looked between them. Wild blackberry pie juice stained Josiah's once pristine clothes.

Malcolm sat clean and neat, an empty plate waiting beside him for a slice of pie he'd never get. Which did she prefer, a quiet man with workman's hands, or a fine gentleman with clean fingernails? She saw Pa heading toward them.

"I appreciate the qualities both of you have," Sally said slowly. "You're both businessmen who care for those in need in your own ways. I realize you're offering me a beautiful life, Josiah, with plenty of fashionable hats, but I've decided I'm really a sunbonnet girl. There's no question in my mind."

Malcolm slowly lifted his head as understanding dawned, and his well-loved face split into a grin. Ewan's sweet fiddle began the Virginia Reel. Children ran among them piping their flutes; the dog lifted his now purple muzzle to howl.

"Choose your partners," Ewan called from the church steps.

Malcolm rose and bowed. "A hard-working sunbonnet girl you are."

Sally curtseyed.

"May I have your hand?" He colored. "I mean, may I have this dance?"

She laughed, joy filling her soul, and she placed her hand in his. "The answer to both is yes."

He led Sally to the dance area and looked deep into her eyes. "I would like to work with and for you always. Will you marry me?"

Sally tilted her head. "You're not so tongue-tied now."

"No. Will you?"

"Yes."

Ewan's fiddle set their feet, and hearts, a dancing.

And not once did Sally's sunbonnet slip off her head.

Michelle Duval Ule is the daughter of a businessman and a teacher. A native of San Pedro, California, she learned to sew at a young age and for many years only wore dresses made by her seamstress grandmother. She and her family live in Northern California where she dances Zumba most mornings. You can learn more about her at www.michelleule.com.

You also can read about Ewan and Kate's musical courtship, as well as Malcolm learning math, in Barbour Publishing's *The Yuletide Bride*, part of *The Twelve Brides of Christmas* collection. Find out more here: www.12Brides.com.